When a DUKE DESIRES *a Lass*

A SWEET REGENCY HISTORICAL
SEDUCTIVE SCOUNDRELS, BOOK FIFTEEN

COLLETTE CAMERON

Blue Rose Romance®

Sweet-to-Spicy Timeless Romance®

"What are ye afraid of, lass?

"What has kept ye a prisoner, afraid to live your life?"

Seductive Scoundrels
A Diamond for a Duke
Only a Duke Would Dare
A December with a Duke
What Would a Duke Do?
Wooed by a Wicked Duke
Duchess of His Heart
Never Dance with a Duke
Earl of Wainthorpe
Earl of Scarborough
Wedding her Christmas Duke
The Debutante and the Duke
Earl of Keyworth
Loved by a Dangerous Duke
How to Win a Duke's Heart
When a Duke Desires a Lass

Check out Collette's Other Series
Daughters of Desire (Scandalous Ladies)
Highland Heather Romancing a Scot
The Blue Rose Regency Romances:
The Culpepper Misses
Castle Brides
The Honorable Rogues®
Heart of a Scot

Collections
Lords in Love
Heart of a Scot Books 1-3
The Honorable Rogues® Books 1-3
The Honorable Rogues® Books 4-6
Seductive Scoundrels Series Books 1-3
Seductive Scoundrels Series Books 4-6
The Blue Rose Regency Romances-
The Culpepper Misses Series 1-2

Dedication

For every loyal reader who has enjoyed

my Seductive Scoundrels Series.

I hope the romances and the characters

brought you hours of enjoyment and entertainment.

Thank you, and God bless you.

1

Hyde Park – London, England

23 April 1811

Head bent and deep in thought, Emily Grenville briskly strode Hyde Park's footpath. Circumstances forced her to take her daily constitutional at the ridiculously early hour of eight every morning, beginning at Grosvenor Gate.

Wrapped in her tangled reflections and a new velvet redingote, she walked alone.

Being alone doesn't equate loneliness, she told herself for the umpteenth time.

Neither did being surrounded by people shield one against loneliness.

A truth she'd endured for several years with a valiant smile, demure responses, and a battered heart. Only, of late, she'd found it harder and harder to accept her fate—not a destiny of her choosing but one which had been thrust upon her by another's callous choices and deeds.

Raising her head, Emily scanned the pathways and greens. Ducks swam contentedly in the Serpentine, quacking every now and again. Soon there would be downy brown and yellow ducklings trailing their watchful mothers or sunning themselves on Duck Island.

A lone rider entered the park on the far side, and a pair of women in humble attire hurried along another path, likely to their places of employment.

In general, *le bon ton* denizens eschewed rising early, let alone taking the air at this hour. Which meant no obligatory exchanges of banal pleasantries and disingenuous smiles. Emily needed this tranquil time to herself and preferred the solitude.

Besides, it wasn't as if she was a dewy-eyed innocent, fresh from finishing school, or a debutante requiring a chaperone to ensure she wasn't despoiled or her reputation tarnished. Thirty and widowed, Emily answered to no one but herself, which suited her fine.

Walking cleared her mind, invigorated her, and truth be told, gave her something to fill one of the many empty hours that occupied her days. After her niece and ward, Justina, married the Duke of San Sebastian, and they'd invited Emily to live with them, she had far too much free time on her hands.

Unaccustomed to idleness, of late she'd begun contemplating that it might behoove her to remove herself to her small cottage in Bristol to rusticate or perhaps become a traveling companion to an elderly dame. Justina would undoubtedly object—strenuously—so Emily kept those possibilities to herself.

Emily had discreetly registered with two agencies to test the waters regarding a companion position. It couldn't hurt to see what might be available. *If* she decided to strike out on her own again.

Her half boots struck the pavement with a satisfying *click-clack, click-clack* as she marched along, swinging her parasol in time to her gait. In the morning's hush, the sharp snap of her heels carried along the solitary path, and a squirrel raised its bushy red tail, flicking the appendage in agitation.

At Emily's approach, the panicked creature darted across the path and up a tree, where another squirrel raucously scolded from a branch extending a few feet over the pathway. A grayish-brown turtle dove swooped low and landed in the lush spring grass. Its mate gracefully soared to a spot nearby and cooed a greeting.

A nascent smile tipped Emily's mouth.

Even the birds and squirrels had mates.

Emily didn't envy them.

Indeed not.

She'd tasted matrimonial bliss for a brief spell— two whole months to be precise—and that had been enough for her. Despite a half-dozen marriage proposals since entering widowhood, she eschewed any mention of marriage in connection with her name.

Never mind that the "matrimonial bliss" rendition wasn't *precisely* the truth. Regardless, that was the respectable version Emily had told others for many years, and repeating it had become a habit. That, too, was a protective shield against disgrace and *on dit*. She prayed wagging tongues never latched onto the truth.

That she had, in fact, never legally been Mrs. Clement Glenville. Rather hard to be a man's wife when he already possessed one who was very much alive.

Picking up her pace, Emily inhaled deeply, appreciating the blossoming trees' faint fragrance. Normally, London stank, and the perpetual pewter clouds and coal dust, lying like a thick mantle upon the city, enhanced the cloying stench.

She preferred coastal breezes and tangy air to the stale stuffiness of London.

Today, she wrestled with a rare fit of the blue devils.

Perhaps seeing Justina and Baxter so deeply in love stirred dormant longings. Made Emily wish for what could never be. Nevertheless, wallowing in self-pity had never been her way. Instead, she focused on her blessings.

Enjoying God's creations and nature's beauty did much to dispel her baffling doldrums. She had much to be grateful for, so why, with each passing week, did discontentment raise its gnarled little head higher and higher?

It was becoming more and more difficult to tamp down her restlessness and she felt herself slipping into vulnerability. An untenable state she vowed to avoid at all cost.

It was enough to see Justina happily married to a good man, as were most of Justina's girlhood friends—therefore Emily's friends by default. All had wed to surprisingly decent fellows, everything considered.

Conceding that some men ranked above truffle hogs and clatterfarts was a step forward for Emily. Not so long ago, she'd believed all males were charlatans, scapegraces, and opportunistic bounders. The late Lieutenant Clement Grenville most assuredly had been.

She hadn't learned the depths of Clement's treachery until it was too late. Until he'd destroyed her trust in men forever. How he had whispered words of love and devotion and rattled off colossal lies with the same tongue still confounded her.

Bah.

Resolutely shoving the unpleasant ruminations to a fusty corner in her mind, Emily gripped her parasol's black carved handle and gave the accessory a rather vicious swing. She *would* enjoy this outing—would cherish the glorious break in the weather and a chance to clear her head.

A vibrant azure sky and effervescent sunbeams filtering through trees laden with leaves and buds testified to the unusually passive spring weather. Ensconced in this mazarine-blue velvet redingote—another gift from Justina and quite the loveliest thing Emily had ever worn—she felt like an impostor.

A charlatan herself.

She appeared poised, wealthy, privileged…none of which were accurate.

If people, specifically, the *ton,* knew the truth—knew that Emily's marriage to the lieutenant had been a diabolical sham… Clement had kept her ignorant of that particular and rather critical detail, the blackhearted bigamist.

A shudder rippled from Emily's waist to her nape.

The *on dit* would be ruinous.

Only Justina was privy to the whole sordid tale, and she would never breathe a syllable.

As Emily continued along the footpath, another rider, two nurses pushing prams, and a trio of bewhiskered elderly gentlemen appeared. Others had likely ventured forth to take the air this fine spring morning, but she couldn't see them from her vantage point.

Another horse burst into the park, its rider obviously struggling to control the large mount. Lifting a hand to her bonnet's brim to shade her eyes, Emily squinted into the sun's brightness. A playful breeze teased the curls framing her face and the loosely tied azure ribbon under her chin.

Black mane and tail flying, the gray tore down the pathway she stood upon rather than take to Rotten Row as the other equestrians had.

Her heart skipped a beat, then another.

Surely the horseman would turn his mount aside.

Wouldn't he?

A long-ago memory struggled to the surface of Emily's mind. One she'd buried under pain, sorrow, time, and pure determination to not recollect.

She'd been six and playing a few feet away from her mother as they watched Emily's father atop a new stallion. Something—she never knew what—had spooked the massive beast, and the horse had bolted.

Mindless with terror, the wild-eyed animal had charged straight at Emily.

Acrid terror clawed at Emily's throat as it had that dreadful day, and she broke into a fear-induced sweat. Every limb seemed weighted by stone, and she could not move.

Not again.

As she had all of those years ago, Emily froze, petrified to the very marrow of her bones. Unable to inhale, unable to look away, unable to move a single muscle, knowing, *knowing*, she was about to die.

God help me, Emily mouthed, but no sound escaped her parted lips.

She heard her mother's rasping, strangled gasp of fear. Felt Mama roughly seize her and throw her to the side. Heard Mama's godawful shriek, cut short by the stallion's impact.

Papa cursed and shouted, and then... *and then...* another sound resounded...

A hard, sickening thud.

That wretched day had orphaned Emily, altered the course of her life forever, and left her with a fear of horses she'd never overcome.

She struggled to inhale.

Commanded her leaden feet to move.

Move. Move. Move.

Nothing.

"Are ye daft woman? Run!"

A man's hoarse shout shook Emily from her hypnotic stupor.

The rhythmic pounding of feet and a man swearing beneath his breath gradually filtered through her muffled hearing.

The horse and rider were almost upon her.

Face waxen, eyes wide with dread, lips pulled into a tense, determined line, and a hand fisted in the horse's ebony mane, a young man bent low over the horse thundering toward Emily. He'd lost the reins but tried valiantly to grasp one, almost falling from the saddle in his efforts.

A moment later, something—not the horse?—

plowed into Emily, knocking the breath from her lungs and her feet from beneath her. She landed partially on her side and partially on her back in the grass beside the path.

Sweet Jesus on Sunday.

Had she broken a rib?

A large, heavy, *male* form lay atop her, nearly suffocating her.

The horse thundered past, so near she felt the wind against her exposed legs.

Exposed?

Well, at least there wasn't a crowd to witness her mortification and ignominy.

Emily tried to move but groaned and ceased when pain shot through her hip and shoulder. No doubt about it, she'd be covered in bruises and possibly had suffered a broken bone or two given the size of the behemoth pinning her to the ground.

A surprisingly pleasant-smelling behemoth.

She inhaled.

Sandalwood, cedar, and perhaps cloves? Or was it carnation?

Are you mad, Emily?

She'd nearly been run down, and she lay beneath a stranger contemplating the pleasantness of his cologne?

Cracking an eyelid open, she carefully turned her head, waiting for pain to stab her again. None did. Her gaze collided with familiar piercing blue eyes, the color of summer sky, beneath slashing dark-auburn brows.

A groan lodged in her throat.

Really?

Him?

That clot head had to be her savior?

2

Tobias Forsythe, Duke of Heatherston's strong mouth quirked into that disarming smile he bandied about with the ease of a baker kneading bread.

When had he come to Town?

"You?" Emily croaked, whether because of his great weight pressing into her, fear having tightened her throat, or shock at unexpectedly seeing him, she couldn't discern.

"'Tis a great pleasure to see ye again, Mrs. Grenville."

He'd slipped into his Scottish brogue, and the burr tunneled deep into her belly, warming her in a most peculiar fashion. Almost as if her femineity responded to him.

Stuff and nonsense. What utter rubbish.

Clutching as much of her tattered dignity as Emily could muster—given she lay beneath the duke with her legs bared, and she was quite certain the scant few people in Hyde Park had homed in on her circumstance and were approaching with alacrity an Ascot racehorse would envy—she managed with a flat look, "I cannot say the same, Your Grace."

Throwing his head back, his strong chin on full display and exposing the thick column of his throat, Heatherston burst into laughter.

What was so dashed humorous?

His slightly too-long auburn hair fell forward over his forehead when he lowered his head once more, his bachelor-button-blue eyes alight with hilarity.

"Are ye hurt, lass?"

Genuine concern shadowed his eyes rimmed with lush lashes many a woman would envy.

Emily did, and envy was far too pedestrian for her.

"I don't think so." Emily pulled in a shallow breath. "But as you are squashing me, I cannot be absolutely certain."

A deep melodic chuckle reverberated in his much too wide and hard chest.

With admirable agility and adeptness, he bounded to his feet and then held out his hand. He didn't even glance at Emily's legs, which were, as Emily feared, bared to mid-thigh.

"Permit me to assist ye to your feet, Mrs. Grenville."

His gentlemanly behavior warmed her heart in a strange manner, and that he hadn't leered at her legs raised him a notch in her estimation. Though he still ranked among the slithery, crawly creatures; maggots and the like.

Avoiding his keen gaze, Emily pushed her skirts down, silently bemoaning the grass stains that marred her gown and redingote. As she accepted his hand and rose, she reminded herself that they were only things— *but such beautiful new things.*

"Thank you, Your Grace."

A quick glance around revealed concern stamped upon the faces of a half-dozen people.

His grace released her hand but remained near as if

he feared she'd swoon.

Emily was made of more starch than that, but she didn't blame him for being cautious. After all, she'd have had sufficient time to move out of the horse's path if she hadn't been transfixed with terror.

"I'm quite fine," she assured the small crowd with a smile that wasn't as steady as she wished. Swiping at the blades of grass and dirt clinging to her garments and ruining her gloves in the process, she said, "Just a bit bruised and smudged."

She raised her soiled dark-blue gloves—a new pair purchased just last week to match her redingote—and grimaced. Frugal to the point Justina had called her a pinchpenny, Emily abhorred waste.

Heatherston silently handed her parasol over.

"You gave me quite a start." A plump nurse with a kindly face gently bounced the pram before her where a wide-eyed toddler lay, sucking his thumb. "I was certain you'd be run down."

"She would've been if his grace hadn't been so quick on his feet." Wearing an alarmingly ugly tweed suit, a shade between vomit and pond scum, a skinny fellow straightened his bowler hat. "Well done, sir."

How could he have known Heatherston was a duke?

"Hear, hear," the trio of gentlemen sporting unfashionable muttonchops and wearing almost identical black striped suits intoned with enthusiastic nods. Bankers, she'd wager. Exchanging jovial grins, they shook each other's hands as if they'd prevented Emily from being trampled.

Hoofbeats approaching at a sedate pace echoed nearby.

As one, the small crowd turned to where the runaway horse and rider advanced at a serene gait. A far cry from the out-of-control beast that had thundered by mere minutes ago. However had the horseman managed to rein the stallion in?

Their return was unexpected but not unwelcome.

Emily had expected both to be halfway to Green Park by now. Or the other side of London. It showed courage and decency to return to the scene where you'd nearly trampled someone.

Shamefaced and still rather pale, the youth glanced

between Emily and the duke and then settled his attention on Emily again.

"I'm awfully sorry, miss." The young man cut Heatherston a fretful glance. "I underestimated Spiorad's stubbornness and determination to take his head. He has a good heart but is a bit hardheaded."

"A lot like ye," the duke muttered beneath his breath as he ran his fingers through the hair at the back of his head.

Tucking his chin to his chest and looking suitably contrite, the youth patted the horse's sweaty neck.

Sweat glistening off his coat, the creature seemed the modicum of docility now.

"Well, I should be going, I suppose. Spiorad could use more exercise." Expertly reining the horse around, the young man made to depart.

"Nae!"

The single syllable cracked through the air like a gunshot.

Heatherston's jaw grew tense, and displeasure shone in his startlingly attractive eyes.

Why was Emily noticing his eyes?

Perhaps she'd hit her head after all and was slightly dazed.

"I warned ye, Avery, not to ride him. Ye could've hurt or killed Mrs. Glenville or Spiorad with your recklessness."

Avery paled and swallowed. Shifting in the saddle, he eyed the small crowd, all of whom leveled justifiable, accusatory glares at him.

"I apologized, Uncle Tobias." Avery thrust his chin out and swept a hand toward Emily. "No harm was done. She's right as rain."

Emily didn't agree with that assessment.

Wait?

Uncle Tobias?

Emily narrowed her eyes and skimmed her glance over the youth. His eyes were the exact same shade of blue as Heatherston's. Unusual, but not remarkable. He wore a nondescript cap shoved low on his forehead, an ordinary, baggy navy woolen jacket, and black breeches tucked into small, knee-high boots.

Emily stifled a gasp.

Women's boots.

How could she have missed something so obvious?

The fair skin? The slim build? The reddish-brown winged brows, almost the same color as her uncle's?

This was no lad but a young lady.

A very *unladylike* young lady from all appearances.

Heatherston sent his commanding gaze around the gawking onlookers. "Thank ye for your concern. It is much appreciated. Ye may be about your business now. As ye can see, all is well."

The duke effectively dismissed them. Hands on his hips, he waited for the spectators to wander away. His pantaloons bore grass stains, but even so, he presented an imposing figure.

An inch or two over six feet, his demeanor and the broad shoulders stretching the fabric of his jacket made him commanding.

Once the curious onlookers had dispersed, the fellow in the tweed suit giving them a lengthy, assessing glance, Heatherston pointed his attention to his niece.

He was furious, but other than the tightening around his mouth, he didn't reveal his wrath.

"Dismount, Avery. Ye aren't riding again until ye learn to respect my directives."

Avery's mouth curved down mutinously, but with an exasperated sigh, she obeyed. Swinging her leg over the saddle, she jumped to the ground.

Arms akimbo, she glared daggers at her uncle. "You are a beast."

He closed his eyes for a second, and Emily would've sworn he entreated the Almighty for strength. Or patience. Or guidance.

Likely all three.

She'd done the same too many times to count while raising Justina, and Justina hadn't the rebellious inclination Miss Avery apparently possessed.

When the duke opened his eyes, something akin to sorrow, or perhaps regret, shone in the blue depths.

"I ken ye don't believe me, but I do what I do because I care for ye, lass."

A sullen pout descended upon Avery's expression, and she snapped, "You would've left me in Aberdeen if you cared for me."

Though her refined voice carried a hint of an accent, it lacked the rumbling burr of her uncle's. She was formally educated, then.

Well, that was something.

"Not by yourself, lass. Ye've spent too much time alone as it is." Though gentle, the duke's response brooked no argument.

Feeling very much the voyeur, Emily cleared her throat. She'd leave them to their family issues and see if her stained garments were salvageable.

"Thank you for your assistance, Your Grace. I'll be on my way now."

"Mrs. Grenville, please allow me to make amends for my niece's…"

He shook his head, causing the wayward gingerish lock to slip farther onto his forehead. It gave him an endearing, boyish appearance.

How old was he, anyway?

"I beg your pardon. Mrs. Grenville, may I introduce ye to my sister's daughter and my ward, Avery Levingtone? Avery, Mrs. Emily Grenville."

"Mrs. Grenville." Avery tilted her head a fraction.

Either she hadn't been taught manners, or she was simply too angry to care about decorum. Emily suspected the latter, and though it was none of her business, she was curious what had triggered such rebellion.

"Avery. That's an unusual given name," Emily ventured in an attempt to lessen the palpable tension.

Her expression arranged into calculated boredom, Miss Levingtone shrugged. "It was my paternal grandmother's maiden name. For reasons I'll never know or understand, my parents thought it an appropriate given name for a girl. They might as well have named me Neale or Dalles for all of the trouble my given name has caused me."

Emily could appreciate the girl's frustration.

"Ye could use one of your middle names." The duke brushed ineffectually at a smear of dirt marking his jacket from elbow to wrist. He glanced up through hooded eyes. "Moira and Yvaine were your grandmothers' names, and both are quite lovely."

"Nae." Miss Levingtone shook her head. "Mama and Papa said they chose my name because they wanted me to grow into a strong, intrepid, and spirited woman. I honor them by using the name they gave me."

Compassion softened the sharply hewn angles of

his chiseled features, and something undefinable stirred in the vicinity of Emily's heart.

He truly cared for his ward.

The Duke of Heatherston was a charming rogue, glib of tongue, quick to laugh, and to Emily's limited knowledge, kind. Last December, she'd rebuffed his interest in her at Theadosia, the Duchess of Sutcliffe's Christmastide house party. However, that had been a protective measure on her part and not a black mark against his character.

She had no more interest in becoming anyone's mistress than marrying again.

"What brings you to London, Miss Levingtone?" Emily asked.

Arms folded and tapping one foot in impatience or annoyance, the girl jerked her chin toward her uncle, all the while giving him the gimlet eye.

"Uncle Tobias insisted I experience a Come Out this Season. He wants me wedded so he can be done with his familial obligation and continue his rakehell lifestyle."

3

Well, Emily had asked, and it seemed that Miss Levingtone was not one to mince words.

Emily quirked an eyebrow toward his grace.

Would he deny his roguish reputation?

"That is not true, Avery."

Heatherston's tone was mild, yet genuine pain threaded his voice and was stamped across his ruggedly handsome features.

Emily almost pitied him, though why should she when *he* wasn't the unhappy orphan standing there?

"I am fulfilling a promise I made to your parents before they died, and I'm not a rakehell."

So he claimed.

Emily eyed the sullen girl. Avery had been orphaned too.

For how long?

Emily's heart went out to the girl. She knew what it was to be an orphan. Also, to be foisted off on a much older brother. A brother busy with his own life and who had no idea what a young girl needed beyond food, shelter, and clothing.

"I vowed I would see that ye had a Season," the duke said, sympathy in his gaze, "when ye were of an appropriate age. Ye might actually enjoy it, Avery, if ye'd let yourself."

What did he, an avowed bachelor, know about a Come Out?

Didn't he know the official Season had already begun?

Emily inspected Heatherston's strained features.

That he loved his niece was obvious, but that he had no idea what to do with a girl on the cusp of womanhood was equally apparent.

"What do *you* know about such matters?" Avery asked bitterly, echoing Emily's thoughts.

"Perhaps I might be of assistance in that regard?"

Emily could've bitten her tongue off. The dratted

appendage seemed to have developed a mind of its own.

Heatherston and Miss Levingtone turned astonished gazes upon her.

Certain she overstepped, yet plowing onward, despite her pulse racing in alarm, Emily touched Miss Levingtone's arm. "I was orphaned at a young age, and my brother, fifteen years my senior, was named my guardian."

Miss Levingtone's mouth sagged, and tears filled her sapphire blue eyes. "Then you understand."

"As much as anyone can, I do," Emily said.

She bent her mouth upward in empathy.

"I also took on the responsibility of my niece when she was orphaned at ten and raised her as if she were my own child, so I understand your uncle's perspective too. Justina married a short while ago, and I find I have excess time on my hands."

Emily faced the duke and, thrusting aside her misgivings and her conscience shouting *don't do it*, said, "Forgive me if I overstep, but I have ample time. If you are in agreement, perhaps I might offer my assistance with Miss Levingtone's preparation for her Season?"

"You…you would do that after I nearly ran you down?"

Mouth trembling with suppressed emotion, such hope shone in Miss Levingtone's incredulous eyes, Emily couldn't hold a grudge. Besides, it wasn't her nature to be punitive.

"It would be a blessing to me as well," Emily assured her. "I'm accustomed to being busy, and my current idleness is somewhat disconcerting. I would welcome the opportunity to be useful."

Rather than a burden, though both Justine and Baxter would vehemently deny any such thing.

"Yes. Yes." Heatherston agreed without hesitation and with more force than warranted. "Yes, we gladly accept your generous offer, don't we, Avery?"

His acceptance ignited a smile on Avery's face. She nodded eagerly and then stunned Emily by hugging her. "Thank you."

"Might I call upon ye this afternoon to discuss the arrangements?" A primal gleam entered the duke's eyes that immediately made Emily suspicious.

"I shall alert Justina to expect you *both* at four."

Emily angled her head. "There is much to do as the Season has already begun."

"I'm aware," Heatherston admitted. "Unfortunately, circumstances prevented us from leaving Scotland as early as I would have liked to have done." He swiped his hair off his forehead and met his niece's impertinent gaze. "We are here now, and that is all that matters."

It was best to ensure the duke understood exactly what Emily offered and what she did not. She met his amused eyes directly, a challenge in hers.

"I'll remind you what I told you last December, Your Grace."

Acutely aware of Miss Levingtone's riveted attention, veering between Emily and the duke, Emily tucked her parasol under one arm. In that disagreeable conversation, she might've referred to preferring to bed a leper.

"Those criteria haven't changed one iota," she said crisply.

"Ye never allowed me to prove I wasn't a leper, lass."

The duke flashed her a blinding grin, all straight white teeth in a sun-browned face, and gave her a brazen wink.

The forward cad.

"A *leper*?" Miss Levingtone giggled, thoroughly enjoying her uncle's discomfiture.

Except he didn't seem all that put upon.

"Oh, that is too judicious," Avery crowed.

"Alas, she broke my heart." Heatherston pressed both black-gloved hands over his heart in the exaggerated way of a stage performer.

Oh, the lying rotter.

This would not do.

Heatherston's dissembling might give his niece the wrong impression. What if she told others there was something between Emily and the duke?

No, that would never do.

Emily held up her hand, palm outward.

"I shall help Miss Levingtone with her Come Out if you agree to keep our interactions strictly professional."

"Mrs. Grenville, don't ye ken by now? I'd agree to anything ye asked of me just for the privilege of your pleasant company."

Miss Levingtone giggled again. "This is going to prove quite entertaining, I think."

With a will-you-never-cease glare, Emily pursed her lips. She'd brought this upon herself with her generosity of spirit. Pray she didn't regret her impulsiveness sooner rather than later.

"Good day, Your Grace. Miss Levingtone."

With a curt dip of her chin, she bid them farewell.

As she marched away, back stiff as a broomstick and heart beating an unacceptably excited staccato, the duke called, "We shall see ye at four, Mrs. Grenville. The ensuing hours shall be intolerable. Nonetheless, somehow, I shall survive."

Miss Levingtone burst into peals of laughter, and her uncle's deep baritone soon joined in the jollity.

What had Emily done?

"I'm out of my deuced mind."

4

Houghtenwick Hall – Grosvenor Square
London, England
Home of the Duke and Duchess of San Sebastian
Four in the Afternoon

Tobias flipped open the timepiece he'd inherited from his grandfather. Four minutes to four. Perfect. By the time the coach stopped, and he and Avery disembarked and entered the mansion, it should be four of the clock.

Punctuality said much about a person's character and their consideration for others.

Snapping the gold watch closed and returning it to his pocket, he gave Avery a reassuring smile.

This morning when she'd giggled at his teasing Mrs. Grenville, he'd caught a glimpse of the cheerful, carefree lass she'd been until her parents died.

The trouble was, Tobias had no idea what to do to make Avery happy. In point of fact, he had *no* idea what to do with a petulant, defiant eighteen-year-old, much less how to transform her into a debutante.

"Chin up, lass. It's not as if you're entering the dragon's lair."

He gave her another smile meant to reassure her.

Avery didn't return the gesture but instead, presented her profile. Her sullenness had returned almost the instant she'd stopped laughing after Mrs. Grenville's departure this morning.

In truth, Mrs. Grenville had been referred to as a dragon more than once for her diligence in chaperoning her niece, now the Duchess of San Sebastian. She was precisely the sort of woman Tobias could entrust Avery to.

An intelligent, decorous, talented on the pianoforte, but also a kind woman of indisputable character.

Mrs. Grenville's golden curls, big dark jade-green

eyes, rosebud mouth, and delicate features weren't exactly off-putting either. He thought she might be in her late twenties or early thirties.

Far too young to spend her life on the shelf and in the shadow of her niece.

But how to ensure the attractive widow followed through on her offer to prepare Avery for a Season when she held Tobias in such contempt? Simply because he'd dared show that he admired her and would've explored his blooming attraction had she not rebuffed him at every turn.

Mrs. Grenville must've loved her late husband very much indeed.

Something that might've been envy stabbed Tobias sharply behind his ribs.

For the first time in his life, he wondered what it would be like to be adored like that. To have someone love him so much, they were bereft without him.

Until now, he'd not seriously considered matrimony. Six and thirty wasn't so very ancient that he need repine about entering the parson's mousetrap just yet. He'd put off his ducal duty of marrying and securing the dukedom's future this long.

What could it hurt to delay a jot longer?

But Mrs. Grenville had him thinking on marriage more of late. To be more precise, nuptials with *her*.

Certainly not a union with any of the insipid doe-eyed debutantes half his age. As fate—or providence or whatever force had brought the captivating widow into his path—would have it, no woman interested him but the single woman *not* interested in him.

Was that love?

Complex and perplexing?

Was he in love with Mrs. Grenville?

How did one know?

Avery gave a disgruntled sigh and pinched her mouth tighter.

Now wasn't the time to explore the intricacies of infatuation.

In preparation to leave the conveyance, Tobias uncrossed his legs and straightened his top hat. He'd simply have to charm Mrs. Grenville. Persuade her to use her talents on Avery's behalf as she had for her niece, Justina, now the Duchess of San Sebastian.

Tempering his fascination for the widow wouldn't be as easy, but for Avery, Tobias would put aside his own desires.

For now.

Mouth pressed into a mutinous line and arms folded, Avery hadn't spoken two words to him since clambering into the coach without assistance. She hadn't forgiven him for dragging her to London a mere eight months after she'd returned from finishing school. She'd far rather trundle about in boy's garb at Ballyleigh Court, his estate where she'd been raised.

Though Ballyleigh was Tobias's by way of ducal inheritance, his sister, Wynda, and her husband, Seumas, had stewarded the holdings for nigh on a decade before they died five years ago in a freak accident. During a windstorm, a tree had fallen on their curricle, robbing him and Avery of their closest kin.

Tobias supposed he ought to have insisted Avery remain in Scotland and arranged to have a governess or companion or whatever was appropriate for a young girl's chaperone live at Ballyleigh Court.

At the time, consumed with his own grief and

having no notion of what a twelve-year-old—almost thirteen—needed, he'd wrongly assumed school would keep Avery busy and her mind off her horrendous loss. He'd mistakenly believed living at Ballyleigh Court, her childhood home, would be too painful. The memories too vivid and poignant.

He'd been wrong in that regard as well.

Avery had told him her explicit sentiments on both accounts in no uncertain terms many times. As recently as yesterday, when they'd arrived in London to take up residence at his Mayfair house, as a matter of fact.

The truth of it was, Avery hated him. Resented and despised that he'd been named her guardian. She went out of her way to challenge his authority and defy him at every turn.

Tobias had seized Mrs. Grenville's magnanimous offer to help with the Come Out like a starving man would a moldy piece of bread. Extending a benevolence neither he nor Avery deserved, Emily Grenville offered him a way out of the convoluted tangle he'd created.

A way to honor his dead sister's wishes that her only child enjoy a London Season.

From beneath his lashes, he observed his recalcitrant niece.

That Avery had conceded to wear a simple but outdated jonquil calico morning gown with a fern-green spencer proved monumental.

Avis, the kitchen-maid-turned-Abigail, had plaited Avery's long chestnut hair with its glossy accents of cinnamon and nutmeg into two braids and wound them into a simple knot. A straw bonnet trimmed in green ribbon and adorned with two yellow silk roses perched pertly upon Avery's head.

If perhaps not the first tulip of fashion, his niece was presentable.

Avery fiddled with the ribbons of her reticule, more nervous than she'd ever readily admit.

"Just how do you know Mrs. Grenville, anyway, Uncle? She mentioned a house party?"

The coach bounced to a halt, saving Tobias from answering. Not that it was a secret.

The truth of it was, his pride had been rather badly bruised at Emily's icy and unflinching rejection of his regard last December.

Without waiting for the coachman, Tobias opened the door and stepped out. He held the door for Avery but didn't extend his hand. She'd refuse his aid in any event, and he wasn't allowing her to flaunt her rebellion.

For an instant, she appeared slightly nonplussed when he kept his hand at his side. Skewing her mouth into a mocking smirk, she hopped from the carriage like a six-year-old rather than a debutante about to embark upon her first *Le Beau Monde* Season.

Three matrons farther along the pavement frowned their disapproval at her unladylike display. Their expressions transformed to sycophant miens when they recognized him and realized whose house Tobias stood in front of.

The estimable Duke of San Sebastian—also a Scot.

However, from their keen gazes and swiftly exchanged whispers, they couldn't contain their avid curiosity about who Avery was.

They'd learn soon enough.

Forcing his lips upward into a friendly smile, Tobias doffed his hat as they passed. "Good afternoon, ladies. Enjoying a bit of air?"

Ladies Roswell-Whistle, Clutterbuck, and Cricklebottom, if he recalled correctly. They preened under his attention, and bobbed their bonneted heads in affirmation.

Excellent.

Tobias needed every ally he could muster to launch Avery into Society. Extending his arm, he gave his niece a pointed look.

With a scowl and mumbled complaint, she grudgingly slipped her hand into the crook of his elbow. She'd been taught proper comportment but thus far, had been mulishly stubborn about displaying decorum.

As they ascended the spotless stairs, the impressive front door swung open.

"Your Grace. Miss Levingtone. I am Bevels." Despite his austerity, kindness warmed the butler's gaze before he bowed, then stepped aside for them to enter.

"Good afternoon, Bevels."

Tobias handed over his gloves and hat, which the servant placed upon a marble-topped half-table situation to the right of the door beside a carved burgundy tufted bench. A matching bench was situated beneath a country picnic painting in a gilded frame across the foyer. A pair of rosewood end tables, topped with lush bouquets of fresh flowers, flanked the second seat.

"Mrs. Grenville and her grace await you in the drawing room." How he managed to keep any inflection from his tone was laudable, though mildly eerie. "Follow me, please."

Without waiting to see if they obeyed, Bevels proceeded down the parqueted corridor at a measured pace. His arms moved in perfect synchronization with his steps.

Step. Swing. Step. Swing.

Did majordomos ever do anything without precise movements?

A shock of pewter hair the butler had failed to tame with pomade stuck out at the back of his head and bounced up and down with each restrained movement, giving him the appearance of a rooster in a tailcoat.

Avery pinched Tobias's arm and speared him with a panicked glance. She mouthed, *"Her Grace?"*

"No need to fret," he assured her in a hushed tone. "I've met the duchess on multiple occasions. She's not much older than ye and is a gentle, kind person."

The dubious sideways glance Avery shot him said she didn't believe a word.

She'd have to see for herself then.

A few moments later, Bevels stood at the drawing room entrance.

"His Grace, the Duke of Heatherston and Miss Levingtone," he announced in a modulated tone.

Radiant in a pale peach gown, trimmed in ivory lace and silk rosettes along the hem, Mrs. Grenville stood speaking to her niece near the window. The light streaming through the glass cast her in an ethereal glow, and Tobias was struck dumb by her incandescent beauty for an instant.

No evidence of her fall earlier today remained, though she might—probably did—sport a few bruises.

When she glanced up and their eyes met across the room, his heart stalled for a full beat.

Emily Grenville alone turned him into a fumbling, incoherent fool.

"Uncle?"

Avery's troubled voice coming from a hazy

distance brought Tobias back to himself. A flush seared his neck that she'd caught him gawking.

Devil take it.

He bowed. "Your Grace. Mrs. Grenville."

The Duchess of San Sebastian glided forward, her face wreathed in a welcoming smile.

"Heatherston. I cannot tell you how pleased I am that Aunt Emily is to assist you in Miss Levingtone's Come Out. You could have no one better to aid you. I shall, of course, be delighted to aid in any way I can too."

Avery had the good sense to curtsy, and quite prettily too.

Tobias could thank the expensive finishing school for that small favor.

Lest he reveal his admiration for Mrs. Grenville, with an alacrity that bordered on terse, he introduced the women to one another.

The duchess reached for Avery's hand. "My aunt tells me you too are an orphan, Miss Levingtone. We've much in common, and I hope we shall become the best of friends."

"Thank you, Your Grace. You are most kind." Avery's unease seemed to melt away, and she gifted Tobias a rare smile as the duchess led her to a sage-green velvet settee.

A silver tea service, four rose-covered china teacups and saucers edged in gold, and three full plates of dainties and pastries had been artfully arranged on the low mahogany tea table.

"You must call me Justina, and I shall call you Avery. Such a lovely name. Our given names quite set apart from all of the Marys, Elizabeths, Janes, and Anns, do they not?"

"Indeed, Your Grace," Avery readily agreed.

Tobias could've hugged the duchess for turning Avery's unusual name into something to be admired rather than scorned or cause embarrassment.

"I have already determined that my daughters, should I be blessed with any, shall have original names." Her grace lifted the teapot with practiced ease. "Let's have a cup of tea and discuss what would make an ideal Season for you, Miss Levingtone. I'm sure you have many ideas. I think it best to consider the debutante's preferences whenever possible."

Very clever of the duchess to make it perfectly clear Avery's Come Out was about her and not what others wished to impose upon her.

Mrs. Grenville approached, her earlier irritation with Tobias masked by her usual, pleasantly benign expression. "Your Grace."

The slightly husky edge to her voice was at odds with her poised perfection.

She dipped a shallow curtsy, and Tobias answered with another brief bow.

A slight flush mounted her smooth, sloping cheeks.

Perhaps she wasn't as impervious to him as she pretended.

She'd restyled her hair and left a few longer curls to frame her face, and one longer curl teased her shoulder. Pearl earrings hung from her dainty earlobes, and a single strand of pearls encircled her neck.

Classical and refined, not garish and overstated.

Her jewelry was a reflection of her.

Mrs. Grenville—Emily—for Tobias could call her Emily in his thoughts, could he not? wore no gloves.

Not for the first time, he noted the absence of a wedding ring or any indication she'd worn a ring recently.

Wouldn't she yet wear her late husband's ring if she still grieved the man?

"Shall we join our nieces, Your Grace, or would you prefer a more private discussion?"

Her gaze strayed to a pair of chairs situated before another window that would afford them a degree of privacy yet still remain respectable.

As much as Tobias was tempted to snatch a few moments alone with Emily, this was not the time. Besides, alone was an exaggeration with their nieces only a few feet away. They'd have plenty of opportunities for confidential *tête-á-têtes* over the coming weeks.

His heart knocked against his breastbone in anticipation.

"I think we must join them," he said, hoping his voice didn't reveal his reluctance. "I don't want Avery to feel left out of any decision-making."

"Quite right." Approval flickered in Emily's eyes, and she offered him a genuine smile.

"As ye may have gathered, she's not altogether keen on having a Season," he said.

"That can change." Emily angled as if to join the other women.

"I would beg a moment, please, Mrs. Grenville."

After a swift glance toward Avery and the duchess absorbed in conversation, she met his eyes, a question in hers. "Yes?"

How Tobias longed to take her delicate hands in his, to brush his lips across the back. But he must tread carefully this go-round. He'd been too bold, too confident in his approach before.

Emily was as skittish as a wild mare, and he'd frightened her. Yes, subtlety was a much better strategy if he wanted to gain her trust and friendship. Hopefully something more too.

But for now, he'd honor her request to keep their relationship unromantic. Once Avery had been launched into Society, however…

Tobias offered a neutral upward sweep of his mouth. "I wanted to make certain ye haven't any injuries from…"

"You plowing into me with the force of a draft horse?"

For once, she appeared amused rather than annoyed. A smile played around her pink mouth, and her eyes sparkled with something other than ire.

"Precisely." He grinned, dumbfounded at how a simple smile from her made him ridiculously lighthearted and optimistic.

"You needn't concern yourself on my account, Your Grace. I am quite recovered. My pride and body suffered a few bruises, but I cannot fault you for my foolishness. I should have run."

"Why didn't ye?" Tobias searched her face, not missing the shadow that descended, stripping her earlier humor.

She sent a guarded glance toward the Duchess of San Sebastian and Avery.

"It wasn't the first time I was nearly run down by a horse." She turned her focus aside for a moment, her gold-tipped lashes caressing her alabaster cheeks. "When I was six, a stallion my father had recently acquired nearly trampled me."

No wonder she'd frozen—petrified.

Even after all this time, sorrow tightened her mouth and darkened her eyes to indigo.

She drew in a ragged breath, and her voice, a mere thread of sound, said, "My mother just managed to shove me out of the way in time, but she wasn't as fortunate. She saved me, to her own peril. After the impact, the horse threw my father."

She raised tumultuous eyes to his, and the pain there cleaved his chest.

"They both died before my eyes."

Jesus, Joseph, and Mary.

Tobias was halfway to reaching for Emily, to pull her into his arms in a comforting embrace before he caught himself. Instead, he touched her upper arm, wishing with all of his heart he had the right to soothe her.

"I'm truly sorry, Emily. That's not sufficient for such a loss, I ken."

Inhaling a deep breath, she hitched a shoulder and summoned a brave face.

How he admired her courage and fortitude.

"It was a long time ago, and it rarely affects me as it did today." She slid another glance toward her niece and Avery. Fingering the pearls at her delicate collarbone, she puzzled her brow.

"Tell me, Your Grace, when did Miss Levingtone lose her parents? How old was she?"

Tobias brushed his fingertips across his forehead. "A little more than five years ago. A tree fell on their curricle. They died instantly. Avery was twelve, almost thirteen, at the time."

"She's still quite angry, isn't she?" No judgment or condemnation, but rather understanding and empathy tempered Emily's tone.

Tobias couldn't hide his surprise at her insight.

"Very. At her parents. Me. God." Shrugging, he quirked an eyebrow. "Life in general."

Emily slowly nodded. "We shall need to be careful how we approach her Season then. I think a private conversation between us is in order after all."

"Where and when?"

Bollocks.

He needn't seem so eager.

Desperate was more accurate.

"Are you two going to stand there talking in hushed tones the whole while?" the duchess asked with the slightest hint of disapproval.

Her gaze vacillated between Tobias and her aunt.

Drollness tilting her mouth the merest bit, Avery assessed him and Emily too closely for his comfort.

"Not at all," Emily said with a radiant smile.

Under her breath, she whispered, "Tomorrow. Hyde Park at eight," before joining the other women.

It wasn't a clandestine rendezvous, *per se,* but Tobias couldn't prevent the thrill of expectation sluicing through him as he took a seat and accepted a cup of fragrant, steaming tea.

With luck and a great deal of favor from the Almighty, he just might accomplish his goal of launching Avery successfully into Society and simultaneously wooing the reluctant widow.

Near Hyde Park

The next morning

Emily released an audible, irritated huff when she had to slow her steps for the third time in as many minutes. Though subtle and assuredly not comment-worthy, her public display of temper earned her an inquisitive look from a young lad dashing past.

She was *not* eager to see the Duke of Heatherston again.

Nonetheless, her dratted feet conspired with her erratic pulse to rush her along. It would not do for the duke to think she *wanted* to see him.

Don't you?

No. Not like *that*.

Never like that again.

Exchanging vows with a man already married and the father of three children who deserted her in a foreign country…well, that treachery tended to put a woman off men and marriage for a lifetime.

Never mind that Clement had vowed undying love for Emily.

His excuses for his unforgivable ploy still rang in her ears.

My wife is an impossible shrew.

I must think of my three children.

How amazing that he could remember his children *after* he'd knowingly deceived Emily and not only proposed but had the gall to marry her under false pretenses. The reprehensible bounder. All the while knowing, *knowing* by heavens, he'd have to abandon her at some point.

Leave her.

Ruined. Alone. Destitute and devastated.

Praise God she hadn't been with child, and her diplomat brother Richard had requested she once more act his hostess until he died unexpectedly. Circumstances had brought Justina to her doorstep a short while later, and that had been the greatest blessing for the past decade.

Now Emily had been given a new purpose. Help Avery Levingtone prepare for her Come Out.

Yes, it was only for a short while. The task wasn't glamorous or life-changing, except for perhaps Avery. Regardless, it made Emily feel needed and valuable. Not that Justina and Baxter made her feel inadequate or unwanted.

Indeed, they couldn't be kinder, more accepting, inclusive, or loving.

However, for almost a decade, Justina had been Emily's focus. Her niece had filled the gaping void Clement's perfidy had left. These next few weeks, assisting Avery Levingtone would be a temporary reprieve.

Emily knew that.

But she could use the time to decide her future and what that looked like.

Elbows linked, two giggling maids hurried past,

baskets on their arms. Probably headed to the market for their household.

Emily glanced up, and her breath hitched.

Arms and ankles crossed and leaning indolently against Hyde Park's entrance, waited the disarming Duke of Heatherston. Neck bent as he studied the mundane path, he hadn't spotted her yet.

She allowed herself a moment to take him in from the long, lean legs encased in black pantaloons tucked into shiny Hessians. He wore a charcoal-colored coat and a gray and burgundy striped waistcoat. Straying from typical fashion, a neatly tied maroon neckcloth encircled his neck. His gray beaver hat with grosgrain ribbon shadowed his angular features.

Unlike many of his peers, he didn't carry a walking stick.

He appeared deep in contemplation.

What held his attention so rapt?

If she could ever trust again…*if* she hadn't built fortified battlements of protection around her heart, she might've been tempted to explore her interest in the enigmatic duke.

But then again, her judgment in men was sorely inadequate.

As if sensing her perusal, Heatherston glanced up.

His piercing cobalt gaze landed on her, and she felt the force of the impact as surely as if he'd reached across the distance and touched her.

She'd heard ridiculous drivel about time hanging suspended and the world diminishing until only two people existed from books and even a few tittering women. Never could Emily have believed there was any truth to the nonsense.

Except, at this moment, her gaze meshed with the duke's, his spirit touched hers.

Or perhaps hers touched his.

It mattered not.

What did matter was there wasn't an explanation for this scintillating current pulsating between them. An electrical charge lifted Emily's nape hair, brought goose pimples to her arms, and arrested her in her tracks to stare in wide-eyed wonderment.

What was *this*?

He slowly straightened and dropped his arms to his

side. Expression befuddled but keenly alert, he returned Emily's undaunted stare.

They both began walking, inexplicably drawn together like magnets. Or the ocean to the shore. Unable to resist the pull, the paranatural attraction.

When Emily stood a mere two feet away, her heart beating as wildly as a trapped bird, she opened her mouth. "I…"

What did she say?

I don't know what this is.

I don't understand it.

It frightens and fascinates me.

The duke rescued her from her tongue-tied discomfiture.

His azure eyes smoldering with something she couldn't identify, he curved that mouth into a roguish grin.

The rake.

She'd be bound that he knew exactly what he did to her.

"Good morning, Emily."

The low, melodic timbre of his voice when he said her name sent a shiver up her spine.

Was it possible to incinerate on the spot?

Never—not even when she'd been married—had she felt this soul-searing, smoldering awareness.

"Your Grace."

Drat her breathiness.

Emily had always disliked her husky voice, but she sounded positively sultry at the moment.

He extended his elbow. "Shall we?"

Emily peered at his arm, uncannily aware that if she touched him, this unfathomable attraction would only magnify.

A welcome breeze whisked by, rousing her from her stupor.

Come now, Emily Cecelia Ann Grenville. You are not a weak-kneed, weak-willed ninnyhammer. Chin up. Marshal your composure.

Filling her lungs with a stabilizing breath, Emily braced herself and slipped her hand into the crook of his elbow.

Other than a slight, wholly tolerable tremor, she angled her head with commendable composure. "Indeed."

They walked in silence for the first few minutes.

Were his thoughts as snarled as hers?

Clearing his throat, the duke glanced downward. "Avery enjoyed herself yesterday. I believe she's quite taken with the Duchess of San Sebastian."

Emily nodded thoughtfully.

"Justina was taken with her as well. I thought luncheon next week with Justina and her intimate circle of friends might be just the thing to introduce Avery. You know them too. It would be a safe environment and establish her in a powerful circle."

"I see ye've thought this through." The duke's features softened with what she thought might be gratitude. "I appreciate it. I confess I've been at a loss how to prepare her for a Come Out."

Emily's heart turned over.

Tobias cared for his niece—wanted what was best for Avery.

"We'll start with the luncheon. In the meanwhile, Avery shall need an appropriate wardrobe for a Season. With your permission, I shall set up appointments with the modistes, milliners, glovers…"

She gave a self-conscious laugh for prattling on. "Well, I needn't name all the merchants."

"Yes, please do make the arrangements. My coach shall be at your disposal." He smiled down at her, and Emily's heart tumbled over itself before resuming an irregular beat.

"Should I plan on accompanying ye?" he asked with commendable sincerity.

Heavens above, no!

Emily almost blurted the blunt refusal aloud.

That would be the epitome of foolishness.

Sitting beside Tobias for hours, selecting fabrics, trims, waiting for Avery's measurements to be taken…Not wise. No indeed.

Emily shook her head, mindful to not seem too reluctant.

"No. It's a tedious process, and I cannot help but think Avery wouldn't appreciate the gesture, no matter how well-meaning." She chuckled and gave him a side-eyed glance. "Most men avoid such excursions. I'm surprised you'd volunteer for that torture."

A relief-filled chuckle escaped him.

"I confess, I wasn't altogether keen on the notion, but as Avery's guardian, I would've put aside my personal discomfiture."

He sincerely did want what was best for his niece.

A little spark ignited in a corner of Emily's heart and warmed her blood, much like sinking into a steaming perfumed and oiled bath.

This was dangerous. Emotions made a woman vulnerable. Hadn't she learned her lesson?

Giving herself a mental shake, she focused on Avery's needs.

"A word in the right ears, namely the duchesses Bainbridge, Sutcliffe, Pennington, Dandridge, Sheffield, Kincade, Westfall, Asherford, Waycross, and Heartwaite; and the countesses of Wainthorpe, Scarborough, and Keyworth, shall ensure numerous invitations to coveted gatherings."

Emily frowned. "However, I don't want Avery overwhelmed."

His forearm tightened for an instant, then relaxed.

"I agree," he said. "Outings to Gunter's, the National Gallery, Covent and Vauxhall Gardens, and the theater prior to balls, routs, and assemblies over the next fortnight will give Avery a chance to assimilate. I honestly don't ken if she likes gatherings or not, or whether she's comfortable in crowds."

A female duck quacked and took to wing with its colorful male in pursuit.

Heatherston watched their flight, then turned and flashed Emily a blinding smile. The corners of his eyes crinkled, reminding her of his usual good humor.

"Emily, might I persuade ye to join me for a coffee, or tea or chocolate if ye prefer, to discuss our strategies further? There's a coffee house, Royale Roast Coffee Shoppe and Café, a few streets away."

He appeared so boyishly expectant that she didn't even scold him for using her given name again as she ought to have done. If someone were to overhear, they would presume a familiarity between Emily and Tobias that did not exist.

Regardless, how could she say no when her heart cried yes? Yes. *Yes.*

Emily feared that the protective fortifications she'd erected around herself were unraveling. No, they were well on their way to tumbling down.

Why didn't she care?

Oughtn't she to be reinforcing her bulwarks and ramparts?

On the other hand, what harm could discussing Avery's Season over a warm beverage do?

In truth, a cup of chocolate sounded divine. Unlike yesterday, today was cool and breezy. Typically fickle April weather, and Emily had become chilled.

She mustn't sound too eager, however. "Yes, that is more practical for planning than strolling in the park, I think."

Tobias shied an eyebrow high on his forehead as if he knew her game but was too polite to comment on it.

"And I cannot stay long," Emily said. It was best to limit their time alone whenever possible. Less chance she'd succumb to something foolhardy. "I promised Justina we'd visit Hatchard's."

Not until this afternoon, but the duke needn't know that detail.

"The booksellers?" he asked. Without waiting for her response, he gave a brisk nod of approval.

"Excellent. That's a perfect start to Avery's introduction to London."

He acted as if she'd included him in the invitation. Which, of course, she had not, and he well knew it.

The rapscallion.

"But…" Scrambling for a feasible excuse to refuse to exclude him and Avery, Emily came up empty. Resigned, she gave him a gimlet glance.

"I cannot decide if that was cleverly done, or not well done of you, Your Grace."

"I ken." He gave her a rakish wink, and her heart toppled over itself.

Lord, I'm in trouble.

6

Mayfair-London

Two days later — Afternoon

Studying the accounting ledger before him, Tobias studiously tried—*and failed*—to disregard the *tick-tock, tick-tock* that recorded each second past two o'clock. The time Emily Grenville was to have met with him to discuss particulars and to devise a plan regarding Avery's Come Out.

Meanwhile, Avery and the Duchesses of San Sebastian, Pennington, and Westfall visited Bullock's Museums of Natural Curiosities at 22 Piccadilly. With their treasure-trove of oddities, the museums were all the rage amongst the *ton*. They provided a perfect opportunity for Avery to be seen publicly without the pressure and expectations of a formal affair.

Avery was sure to be noticed in the company of the illustrious duchesses, and that ought to generate the right sort of invitations.

Egads, he sounded like a bloody pompous snob.

Tobias normally limited his time in England, preferring Scotland. Nevertheless, his commitment to Avery compelled him to put on the pretty and hobnob with London's finest.

Most of whom looked down their pretentious noses at him because he was Scots.

Half Scots. His mother had been Irish. An even greater blemish on his lineage.

The sassenachs could kiss his ar—er—backside.

He speared a glance at the curtain-festooned bay window. A gloaming sky, riddled with pouting charcoal gray clouds, shrouded his view. Blazing logs in the fireplace snapped and sizzled, breaking the monotony of silence and lending a comforting atmosphere to the dreary day.

Pennington's coach had arrived promptly at half-past eleven, and an almost giddy Avery had deigned to give him a hurried peck on the check before flitting down the well-scrubbed steps and boarding the conveyance. The sulky day didn't dampen her cheerful mood in the least.

A nascent smile kicked Tobias's mouth upward on one side.

Despite her determination to spurn her Come Out, his niece was enjoying London.

So was he, by Jove.

Which could be credited to a certain blond-haired, green-eyed spitfire. The perfectly proper Emily Grenville would never admit to the fire smoldering beneath her poise and decorum. Regardless, Tobias had seen the sparks flashing in her eyes. Sensed the embers buried beneath layers of perfected propriety.

Thanks to Emily's grudging invitation, Avery had returned from Hatchard's Booksellers with an array of fashion journals, a gossip rag, and two novels. Yesterday, she'd enjoyed an outing to Green Park. Again with the Duchess of San Sebastian, who seemed to have decided to personally guarantee Avery's resounding success this Season.

Avery had even begun to fret about her limited wardrobe, which was another reason Emily was to meet with Tobias today. Of its own volition, his focus shifted to the mahogany bracket clock atop the carved fireplace mantel, diligently marking each second.

A quarter past two.

Where was Emily?

She'll be here.

He pinched the bridge of his nose and directed his attention back to the tidy rows of figures, each penned with meticulous neatness by his man of business. The numbers blurred before Tobias's eyes as he stared, more troubled by Emily's unpunctuality than he cared to admit.

It wasn't like her to be tardy.

Had something happened?

A broken carriage wheel, mayhap?

Was she ill?

Wouldn't she have sent a note 'round if that were the case?

Of course she would've done.

In truth, she shouldn't be gallivanting around London by herself. Yes, she was a widow, and society's strictures were laxer where widows were concerned. Nevertheless, she was young and attractive. All manner of unsavory sorts prowled London's streets, and a woman alone…

The knocker clacked before Tobias finished the unpleasant thought. He dismissed the coil knotted in his belly as irritation and not fretfulness for her lack of promptness.

A dizzying wave of relief ensconced him.

Thank God.

Slamming the ledger shut, he lurched to his feet, prepared to dash to the entrance, but caught himself before taking a step. In his haste, he bumped the edge of his desk, jangling the top of the gilded bronze inkwell.

No. No.

Control yourself, Tobias admonished sternly.

He mustn't appear overly enthusiastic to see Emily.

The parapets she'd carefully built around herself were beginning to deteriorate and weaken. Soon, they might begin to crumble *if* Tobias trod carefully. One wrong move on his part, and she'd retreat and reinforce her ramparts, and he mightn't ever breach those walls.

In any event, dukes did not answer their own doors.

Unless they were besotted beef-brains.

Compelling himself to return to the chair he'd just vacated, Tobias drew the stack of unopened correspondence closer. The leather he sat upon crackled with his movements. He loathed this part of his ducal responsibilities, but he'd at least look engaged in the mundane task when Pepperford issued Emily into the study.

The knocker rapped again, and he cocked his head, listening for Pepperford's even gait.

Not to worry.

The butler would answer the door in his own good time.

As planned, he'd escort the charming Mrs. Grenville to Tobias's study.

Tobias would order tea (which had already been discussed at great length with Mrs. Cakebread, the cook) and invite Emily to sit on the neo-classical deep green velvet mahogany couch rather than take a chair before his desk.

He could sit beside her on the couch—much more intimate, if somewhat unwise.

Shaking his head, he snorted in disgust.

Look at him.

Pathetic.

Tobias Algernon Florian Forsyth, seventh Duke of Heatherston, acting like a wet-behind-the-ears-milksop at his age. Arranging for tea and plotting seating, all to woo Emily. Without her, naturally, being aware of his machinations.

Surreptitiousness and stealth were key.

"Get a hold of yourself, man." he muttered fiercely, cracking the green wax seal of the first correspondence, another invitation, with his thumb.

He stared blindly at the rectangle.

Always a man who knew his own mind, who made decisions quickly and definitively, Tobias now vacillated like the pendulum in the drawing room's longcase clock.

Back and forth. Back and forth.

Woo Emily.

Focus on Avery's Come Out.

Subtly court Emily.

Avery's successful Season must be my priority.

Marry Emily.

Find Avery a husband.

Avery—Emily.

Emily—Avery.

At this rate, Tobias would end up queer in the attic or seasick.

Why couldn't he do both—sponsor Avery's Come Out and court Emily?

Eyes narrowed, Tobias leaned back and rubbed his nose. Mayhap… He drummed his fingertips on the chair arm in contemplation.

It actually might work.

Yes. Why not?

It needn't be an either-or situation.

In all likelihood, Emily would attend every function Avery did.

He'd insist upon it.

Tobias could kill the proverbial two birds with one stone, and if all went as he hoped it would, everyone would end up happily married before summer ended.

Footsteps sounded outside the open study door.

Emily was here.

He could no more have refrained from training his focus on the doorway than he could reach up and snatch the sun from the sodden, gunmetal-gray sky.

"Mrs. Grenville, Your Grace."

Standing at barely three inches over five feet, what Pepperford lacked in stature, he more than made up in gravity and dignity. His elevated nose gave the impression of at least another two inches in height. A single severe-eyed glance could send footmen and maids scurrying, yet Tobias had never heard the butler raise his voice above a moderated tenor.

Thus far, Pepperford had refrained from turning his censorious gaze upon Tobias but should he ever… Something very near a shiver zipped up Tobias's spine.

God, spare me.

How could someone so diminutive wield such authority, seemingly without effort?

Tobias's attention strayed to Emily, even smaller than Pepperford.

She, too, exerted disconcerting power over him.

He, who stood two inches over six feet and regularly won wrestling matches in Scotland, controlled by that petite bundle of femininity.

If this was love, it turned men into sponge cake.

Unusually flushed and flustered, she hurried forward, untying her straw bonnet's sky-blue ribbons as she advanced. Tension pinched the edges of her pretty eyes and crimped her plump mouth.

"Please forgive me for being late, Your Grace. Something unexpected occurred and delayed my departure."

A hardness he hadn't heard before sharpened her tone.

She was a vision, a breath of fresh air, springtime personified in a white gown with a lace overskirt embroidered with blue forget-me-nots, yellow roses, and pink apple blossoms.

"Please bring a tea tray, Pepperford."

With a slight nod, Tobias dismissed the bland-faced servant. That tea tray would include almond biscuits because they were Emily's favorite.

"At once, Your Grace."

The butler dipped his chin and departed, leaving the study door open in his wake.

Nape hair raised in silent but urgent warning, Tobias moved from behind his desk and approached her.

"Is something amiss, Emily?"

He'd fallen into calling Emily by her given name when they were alone, and she hadn't objected.

She glanced up through her lashes as she set her reticule on the long table behind the couch before removing her bonnet. Wordlessly, she set the hat on a table beside a hand-painted oil lamp and then peeled off her pale-blue gloves.

Patting her golden locks, she angled her head and gave him an indecipherable look.

Alarm bells clanged louder between his ears.

Opening her reticule, she pulled out a neatly folded news sheet. It crackled in protest at being removed from its cozy nest.

"We have a delicate situation, Tobias."

After unfolding the newspaper, Emily handed it to him. Her stomach still churned, and her pulse had yet to return to a sedate cadence after she'd read the small snippet tucked into a gossip column daring to pass as *The Latest Exploits of the Genteel and Fashionable.*

Codswallop and claptrap.

The column was nothing short of mean-spirited speculation and tattlemongering meant to besmirch and titillate.

How any person with a speck of morality or conscience could make a living writing such fabricated and vindictive twaddle, she couldn't conceive. They had much to account for when they stood before the Lord. If

Virgil Smellie, the slimy reporter in his hideous tweed suit, stood before her this minute, she might plant him a facer.

Emily wasn't given to violence. Nevertheless, for Smellie, she'd make an exception.

"What is this?" Pulling his eyebrows together, Tobias eyed the paper in his hand.

She pointed to the passage that had sent her day tumbling teacup over crumpet. "Just there. That bit."

He read the passage aloud.

"In what can only be called uncommon, heroic gallantry, the Duke of Heatherston risked his very life in Hyde Park this Monday past. In danger of being trampled by a runaway horse, his grace threw himself in the path of the savage animal, pushing a lady to safety. This reporter has learned the identity of the most fortunate woman, Mrs. Emily Grenville."

Tobias glanced up, not at all nonplussed. No doubt he believed Emily overreacted.

"It's just trite fluff." He shook the paper, disgust etching his rugged features. "It's a wonder people pay to read this drivel."

"Keep reading." Emily couldn't keep the tension from making her words clipped.

Tobias obliged with a wry quirk of his mouth. He wouldn't think she was overreacting in a few seconds.

"But was his grace truly cavalier and chivalrous, or did he take advantage?"

Tobias's eyebrows snapped together. "What the devil?"

"It gets worse." Emily wrapped her arms around her waist, suddenly chilled despite the spencer she wore.

His frown deepened, and then his eyes went wide as a silent oath slipped past his lips. Tobias gave her a sharp look and then continued reading aloud once more.

"It's not for this reporter to question a peer's intentions, but the other witnesses and I can attest that his grace did not promptly remove himself from Mrs. Grenville's person. Nor did the lady, legs bared to her thighs, attempt to regain her feet as quickly as one in imprudent circumstances might've done.

"To all and sundry, it appeared his grace and Mrs.

Grenville carried on an intimate conversation, oblivious to their, shall we say, compromised position.

"And the horseman, you might wonder? Who was the nefarious villain who so recklessly bore down upon a woman innocently walking the footpath?

"It was no one other than the Duke of Heatherston's niece, Miss Avery Levingtone."

"Bloody, blasted hel—" He broke off mid-word. "Er—I beg your pardon, Emily."

"It's of no consequence." And it wasn't. She wasn't so arrogant as to judge someone for letting a vulgar expletive slip when something vexing happened. She'd leave that self-righteousness for others who were oblivious to the planks in their own eyes.

Staring at the news sheet, Tobias plowed a hand through his hair. Bleakness shadowed his indigo eyes, normally glinting with jollity, when he glanced up.

"Now what?"

"I'm not sure, honestly." Emily lifted a shoulder as she brushed her fingertips across her eyebrows. "My first instinct was that we should all promptly leave London and postpone Avery's Season until next year.

But I had time to ponder during the carriage ride, and…"

Averting her gaze, she caught her lower lip between her teeth, a sliver of uncertainty holding her in check. It would reveal a part of her character she kept hidden beneath the guise of propriety.

"And?" he softly encouraged, taking a step nearer and lifting her chin with his forefinger, compelling her to meet his eyes.

His gorgeous eyes.

Why must they be mesmerizing pools she could get lost in?

He made Emily want to wade straight into those mesmerizing, enigmatic depths and take risks she vowed she'd never take again.

Enough. This was not the time to muddle through her confused emotions.

Shoulders squared, she met Tobias's gaze head-on, certain hers revealed the defiance that had simmered beneath the surface since Clement had tossed her aside like a common strumpet.

"But we did nothing wrong, and I am loath to tuck my tail and run. It implies guilt. Furthermore, mishaps occur all the time with horses, so blaming Avery is beyond the pale. Had you and Avery been commoners, no one would've looked twice.

"I'd like to give that slimy reporter a piece of my mind." Fisting her hands, she firmed her mouth. "No, I'd like to punch him in the nose."

An abashed flush heated her cheeks.

To her surprise, Tobias chuckled that low, melodious rumble that caused her joints to go soft and her insides to grow warm.

"I knew ye had spirit, Firebrand. A flame burns beneath that decorum and politesse."

Emily couldn't prevent her answering grin. "It's my secret. I'll thank you not to bandy it about, good sir."

Tobias sobered, his attention slipping to her mouth.

He wants to kiss me.

And I want him to.

But he wouldn't proceed without her encouragement. Emily knew that as surely as she knew her name was Emily Cecelia Ann Grenville. She'd made her position perfectly clear, and Tobias was an honorable man.

She sidled nearer. "Tobias?"

Primal male understanding caused his eyes to flex at the corners, but he remained silent. He would have her say it, the blasted, obstinate man.

"Tobias?" she said again, her voice huskier than usual.

Emily lifted her mouth in an invitation, unafraid and unashamed. She wanted this. Had wanted it for months, if she were honest with herself. And she always tried to be truthful, no matter how much it hurt or she might regret it later.

She couldn't fight the attraction any longer. "Kiss me. Please."

It didn't matter that the door stood open or that a passing servant would catch an eyeful. It had been so long since she'd been held.

"With the greatest of pleasure, sweetheart."

With what could only be described as a triumphant growl, Tobias gathered her into his arms, and as her eyelids drifted shut, his mouth met hers.

Heat. Warmth. Desire.

All coursed through Emily simultaneously, and she,

who had been married for two months, felt as if this were her very first kiss, it so impacted her.

It exhilarated as much as terrified.

The need to be closer to him was as potent as her need to breathe. Without hesitation, she stood on her tiptoes and wrapped her arms around his strong neck, pulling ever nearer. His clean manly scent, soap, and starched linen teased her nostrils.

Dizzy with desire and a heady, hazy sense of coming home, she clung to him.

How had Tobias become her rock?

A steadying, reassuring, and reliable haven?

Their tongues tangled in a graceful waltz, giving and taking. Seeking and exploring.

Why did he have to be the man who made Emily want things she had forsworn so many years ago? Be the kind of man she could love—might already be falling in love with?

It was impossible.

Her ruinous secret made it so.

She was disgraced, scarcely better than a kept mistress.

He was a powerful and respected duke.

Despondency cooled Emily's ardor, and heart aching, she averted her head.

Tobias pressed her head to the broad plane of his chest, so tenderly and reverently, stinging tears sprang to her eyes.

As if he could read her thoughts and sense her heartache, he murmured, "It's all right, *leannan*."

Leannan?

"We'll take this as slow as ye need."

Tobias dropped a kiss upon her crown, his lips searing Emily, branding her. Making her wish with everything that was in her that she could be Tobias's and cursing Clement Grenville to the lowest level of Hades for robbing her of the opportunity.

Unhurried footsteps and the distinct rattle of a tea tray drove them several steps apart.

Tobias retreated to his desk, and Emily sank onto the couch.

She should tell him there was nothing to take slow, but the words wouldn't form.

The news sheet had fallen onto the cushion, and she

picked it up, seizing the opportunity to change the subject.

Clearing her throat and giving the paper a little shake, Emily asked, "What are we to do about this?"

8

Resting his hips on the edge of the desk and one hand cupping his elbow, the other fisted beneath his chin, Tobias mentally ran through a list of possibilities. As quickly as they formed, he discarded them for one reason or another.

Emily regarded him with patient expectation, as if it were the most normal thing in the world for them to discuss a problem and arrive at a solution together. Something a husband and wife might do.

A hint of color yet tinged her cheeks, and if Pepperford looked closely when he entered the room, he wouldn't miss her residual blush. Or her berry red lips from Tobias's kisses. Nevertheless, Pepperford, being Pepperford, wouldn't betray his observation with as much as a twitch or flared nostril. In truth, Emily could dance on Tobias's desk in her unmentionables, and nothing in the self-possessed servant's demeanor would alter a jot.

Tobias made a mental note to give the majordomo an increase in wages.

A gust of wind sent rain pellets lashing against the window. This April was the ficklest Tobias had ever experienced. One day almost balmy with brilliant blue skies, and the next, raging like a fishwife who caught her husband straying.

Pepperford entered, bearing the tea tray with the dignity of a knight bringing a trophy to his monarch. After setting the laden tray upon the oval table before the couch, he faced Tobias.

"Will there be anything else, Your Grace?"

"Not at present." Tobias straightened and crossed to the sofa. "Thank you, Pepperford."

With another nod, the butler quit the room.

After picking up the scrap of news sheet and setting it on the tea table, Tobias settled beside her.

"Would you please pour, Emily?"

"Of course." The smile teasing the corners of her mouth clearly said she'd already assumed she'd do so.

As she went about the task with practiced efficiency, Tobias hooked an ankle over his knee. He rather liked this intimate coziness that had sprung up between them—could become accustomed to it. To Emily being present in his life.

Waking with her beside him and her beautiful sleep befuddled eyes the first thing he saw each morning. To having her sitting across the table from him at each meal and reading together before the library fireplace in the evening.

And at night?

Egads. Best not to let his mind toddle down that tempting trail.

Emily set the teapot down, and for the first time, Tobias noticed a small scar on her little finger. Though she was a widow, an aura of innocence yet shrouded her.

"How old are you?" he asked impulsively.

"What?" She scrunched her nose in the adorable way she did when perplexed.

He grinned. "How old are you?"

"Don't you know it's rude to ask a lady her age?" She didn't seem particularly offended.

"If I don't ask, how can I find out?" He hitched a shoulder. "I'm six and thirty, by the by."

"Positively ancient," she quipped. "How have you, a duke, managed to avoid the parson's mousetrap for so long?" Abruptly pausing, she shot him a contrite glance. "That was prying. I'm sorry."

"Not a bit of it." Tobias snatched a Shrewsbury biscuit and took a bite. "I haven't met the right woman."

Until now.

An undecipherable expression whisked across her porcelain features. "If you must know, I am thirty."

"Not so ancient," he teased with a roguish wink.

"Ha!" she scoffed, wrinkling her nose. "I'm on the shelf, well and good."

"You're not too old to marry and have children, Emily."

Her features softened with yearning as she stared at the napkin she'd placed on her lap.

"I would like to have had children."

Resoluteness transformed her features. "However,

that ship has not only sailed. It was scuttled and sank to the bottom of the sea."

Wisdom decreed Tobias not push the subject. One that obviously made her distraught.

Look at the progress he'd made already. Emily sat in his office, pouring tea and conversing with him without flinging verbal barbs or skewering him with visual daggers.

Yes, things were coming along splendidly.

"I think we ignore that tripe." Tobias flicked his fingers toward the clipping now lying on the table.

"Really?" She furrowed her forehead, her misgivings on full display. "You think that is wisest?"

He gave a single nod.

"I do. Anything we say in our defense will only fan the gossip—like wind to a fire. It'll give the chinwags a reason to believe there is substance to the twaddle. If *we* ignore it and go on as if ignorant of the rumors, what can anyone say or do? Take the word of a toadying reporter trying to make a name for himself over our powerful circle of friends and me?"

Sugar tongs in hand, Emily chuckled, her eyes

alight with merriment and not umbrage for a change. "I shall concede it's most convenient to have several dukes in your inner circle."

Lord, she was breathtaking when she permitted herself unfettered joy. And it only confirmed what he'd suspected from the moment he'd met her…There was much more to Emily Grenville than she allowed people to know.

"I believe you like three lumps but no milk?" she said.

"Indeed, I do."

So, she'd noticed how Tobias took his tea. Why such a trivial thing should infuse him with satisfaction didn't bear examining. Nonetheless, he tucked that inconsequential detail into the back of his mind.

After adding the lumps, she stirred his tea, then passed him his teacup.

"Thank you." He took a sip before placing the cup on the table.

"I say we increase our outings and attendance." Helping himself to a cucumber and dill tea sandwich, he gestured between them. "We—ye, Avery, and I—shall attend the same functions."

In two bites, he'd consumed the scrumptious morsel.

"I presumed that would be the case," Emily said, adding three almond biscuits to her plate, then tilting her mouth into an abashed smile. "I'm rather fond of almond biscuits."

"I ken." He waggled his eyebrows.

Her fair eyebrows shied high onto her forehead in astonishment. "But how could you?"

"The same way, *leannan*, ye ken that I like three sugar lumps in my tea."

"Oh." She didn't sound entirely convinced. Probably because women were trained to notice such details while most men were oblivious.

While at the San Sebastians' the other day, Tobias *had* observed Emily eating three almond cakes. He asked Mrs. Cakebread to impose upon San Sebastians' cook to share the recipe.

Emily gave him an arch glance—somewhere between amused and cynical before turning the subject back to the matter at hand. "We'll need to see to Avery's wardrobe at once. A heavy purse will ensure the completion of a few gowns is expedited."

"Exactly so." Tobias took another sip, inordinately pleased by her cooperation. "Our smiling, composed presences will quash any unsavory gossip like an ant beneath a boot heel."

Once more, Emily raised a skeptical eyebrow.

"I admire your optimism, Tobias. Even if a trifle misplaced. Surely you know the *ton* believes what the *ton* wants to believe, regardless of facts."

Another blast of wind rattled the windows. The weather grew quite ugly.

"That is true." He rubbed his jaw. "But it is also true that scandals abound amongst the upper ten thousand, and I'll guarantee ye that something more salacious than your bare legs or Avery nearly trampling ye will arise."

"I suppose your confidence is admirable." Doubt tinged the half-compliment.

"I'd wager I'm right." Tobias rolled his shoulder and helped himself to another sandwich. A wicked urge overcame him. "Ye wouldn't care to wager on it, would ye?"

The forfeit when he won could be another kiss.

"Certainly not!" Her affront was genuine. "I do not gamble."

Because she'd needed every half-penny to keep a roof over her and Justina's heads and food in their bellies.

San Sebastian had been helpful in imparting information in that regard.

"I but teased, Emily."

Emily's brow cleared, and she gave him a considering look before nibbling her almond biscuit. "I suppose we shall see and pray you are correct. My main concern is Avery. I don't wish to see her hurt."

"Any more than I do." Tobias sobered, staring into his teacup. "I promised her parents that she would have at least one Season. If she wants to return to Scotland afterward or stay in London, I'll support her."

"Tobias?" Emily notched her impertinent chin upward.

Sudden wariness overtook him. "Aye?"

"About our kiss." She brought her gaze up to meet his. "I must apologize for asking you to kiss me. I said our relationship would be strictly professional, and I overstepped. It was beyond the pale of me."

She would take all of the responsibility upon her small shoulders?

"I didn't mind, lass."

"Well, that was obvious," she retorted with more heat than he'd have expected.

What really went on?

She had regrets. But why?

They shared a pleasurable kiss. Tobias heartily hoped they'd share more in due time.

"Nonetheless, it mustn't happen again. I want to fulfill my commitment to Avery, but I shall have to renege if you cannot promise me that it will not happen again."

Giving her a side-eyed glance, Tobias scratched his forehead.

"Ye want me to promise that ye will never ask me to kiss ye again?"

"No, you obtuse buffoon." Emily dragged in a breath, and something near panic shone in her fern-green eyes. "I want your assurance that you will not kiss me again. That our time together will focus strictly on Avery's Season."

"What are ye afraid of, lass? What has kept ye a prisoner, afraid to live your life?"

"You cross the mark, Tobias," she snapped.

He took her hand in his, cradling it in his palm. "Don't ye ken that I would never hurt ye or let anyone else do so either?"

Mouth slightly parted, she stared at him, vulnerability and distrust fighting for dominance in her eyes.

"I..." She swallowed, the delicate column of her throat working. "I..."

Tobias leaned back against the couch, gently drawing her with him.

She didn't resist.

He *was* making headway with her.

"I vow, I'm a good listener, Emily, and trustworthy."

Tilting her head, she searched his face.

"It's not a pretty tale, Tobias. Nor does it shine a favorable light upon me, my judgment, or my integrity and honesty."

She dropped her gaze to her hand still tucked into his. A ghost of a smile bent her mouth, so sad and fragile that a vice squeezed his heart.

What had happened to make her so distrustful? To have such a low opinion of herself?

"In truth, you may wish to keep Avery from my company when you know the whole of it."

The last came out a meager whisp of sound.

What had reduced his intrepid, courageous Emily to this wounded creature?

"I sincerely doubt that, Emily."

It was too soon to tell her that he loved her—had loved her for months. That nothing she could say or do could purge the love firmly bedded in his heart.

He nudged her chin up with his finger.

"Trust me, sweetheart. I vow, ye'll not regret it."

Presenting her profile, she shifted her attention to the storm brewing outside. Tobias would be bound that an equally fierce tempest raged within her.

He remained silent as the clock counted each passing second.

She must decide she wanted to confide in him without further persuasion.

He wanted her to reveal her secrets because she trusted him. Not because fear or duty or obligation motivated her.

Sighing, she closed her eyes, her golden-tipped lashes fanning across her delicately sloping cheeks.

Eyes still shut, she murmured so softly he had to strain to hear her. "I trusted a man once before and have regretted it ever since."

9

Several interminable minutes slipped by as Emily wrestled with her desire to confess all to Tobias. The wind whipped through the streets, howling as it forced its way between buildings and through cracks. Raindrops attacked the ground with the vengeance of a betrayed lover.

How well she knew that anger and frustration. The helplessness and the fear had become a knotted tangle threaded with half-truths and assumptions.

At one time, long ago before Emily had married a selfish, lying bigamist, she'd trusted so effortlessly. But now, with this honorable man, she feared Tobias's reaction if he learned she'd never been legally wed.

Through no fault of her own, except blindly loving someone, she had no right to call herself Mrs. Grenville.

No right to pretend to be a widow of good repute. It mattered not that Clement had deceived her.

She'd lived with a man, been intimate with him, outside the bonds of matrimony. In the eyes of Society, she was a fallen woman.

What was more—and perhaps was even more galling—Emily had many years to reflect on her gullibility and naivety. About what a gudgeon she'd been.

Scarcely older than Avery, in love with the idea of being in love, she'd not been as wise or cautious as she ought to have been. She agreed to marry Clement too soon. Before she knew anything about him other than how debonair he looked in his scarlet coat and that he kissed divinely.

Worse, however, was the recognition deep in Emily's soul, where she could hardly bear to acknowledge the appalling truth, that what she'd experienced with Clement had been mere infatuation. Not true, abiding love at all.

At times, that truth eviscerated her, made her despise herself for being a fool.

Oh, she'd believed herself wildly, desperately in love with Clement Grenville. Years later, she realized the flighty, powerful obsession had simply been a young, inexperienced girl's first taste of passion at the hands of a skilled seducer.

She inhaled, filling her lungs, welcoming the burn as she held the air there until her pulse steadied, then slowly released the breath.

Perhaps it was better to tell Tobias the truth. Then, if he decided that Emily was unfit to continue helping with Avery's Come Out, perhaps Justina was up to the task. The weight of Emily's guilt and the deception she perpetuated for so long had taken a toll on her.

If that was what he decided, she would accept the offer to be a paid companion that had arrived just yesterday. She'd travel the continent and forget about her tarnished past. *Forget?* No. That might be too optimistic. Perhaps not forget, but at least not have her history haunt her every waking moment.

No matter how far you run, you'll never forget Tobias.

That uncompromising fact could not be denied.

Nor, truth be told, did Emily want to refute it. Despite her determination otherwise, the Duke of Heatherston had penetrated her fortifications.

Her gaze meshed with his, and the reassurance in the depths of his blue eyes made her bold—gave her courage.

In for a penny, in for a pound.

"I met my husband while acting as hostess to my brother, a British diplomat. Clement was a lieutenant in the navy, but he performed many diplomatic duties and rarely went to sea. I always suspected he was a spy. We married after a very brief courtship. When we'd been married two months, he received notice he was being transferred back to England."

She paused, listening to Tobias's breathing. Calm and steady.

The opposite of her irregular heartbeat pounding behind her breastbone and flopping around like a hooked fish.

He didn't urge Emily to go on, seeming to understand that she needed to tell the tale at her own pace, in her own way. To wade through the pain and humiliation that had left her scarred and trepidatious. Feeling soiled, used, bereft, and worthless.

"I assumed I'd go with him or meet him in England later." What loving wife wouldn't have done? "When I asked Clement about the arrangements, he finally confessed he was already married."

Going rigid beside her, Tobias swore in Gaelic. "*Gorach pios de cac.*"

Emily had no idea what he said, but given the granite leaching into his tone, it wasn't repeatable. Regardless, she liked the guttural, lilting quality of the dialect.

Absently fingering the silk frog clasp of her spencer, she recalled that godawful day when her future had shattered. Emily could see it clearly as if it played out before her in this cozy yet masculine study.

Clement's tense jaw and stiff movements as he methodically packed his belongings while she watched mutely—traumatized and devastated. In shock. His appalling absence of empathy for the dreadful situation he'd placed her in. The excuses he expected her to accept, justifying his unforgivable duplicity.

The expectation that she'd simply return to the fold of her brother's household and resume her hostess duties. Even if no one else knew her sin and shame, a soiled dove was still a soiled dove.

Richard would've turned her out onto the street had he ever learned of her ruin.

"Clement had the gall to profess he truly loved me." Emily repeated his pathetic, insulting excuses by rote. "His was an arranged marriage. His wife was a harridan. A shrew. He wished he could be with me, but he had three children to consider."

Her voice, raw and rough, broke.

Yes, *he* had children.

She never would.

What was more, and perhaps the worst of Clement's sins, the mangy cur might've left her carrying his child. He'd given no consideration to that possibility but had discarded her as if he tossed an old pair of boots into the rubbish bin.

Tobias made a soothing sound deep in his throat.

"I don't even know if any of what he told me was true," she whispered, the anguish she'd believed she'd buried rising to the surface once more. "If he was married or had children. He might very well have lied about that too."

Those first months after Emily had returned to England with Justina, she'd been terrified someone would inquire about her married surname, but no one ever had. She supposed the name was common enough that no one had taken notice.

"The bloody scunner." Tobias snaked an arm around her shoulders, pulling her into the comforting shelter of his body. "He deserved to be horsewhipped."

In his anger, Tobias's brogue had intensified.

A log shifted in the fireplace, sending angry orange and crimson sparks flying up the chimney.

How glorious it was to hear someone else speak the truth about Clement and defend her.

"He died before he made it to England," she said.

A queer, twisted sort of justice.

Her brother had been the one to tell her, all the while believing when Grenville reached England, he'd have sent for his bride. Richard had gone to his grave believing that lie.

Emily focused on the blustery weather visible through the window lest Tobias see the embarrassment and regret in her eyes.

"If it were known that I'm not really a widow… I'd be considered a fallen woman. I'd have to leave England lest I bring disgrace upon Justina…Avery." *You.*

"Och. Bollocks to that. Ye were wronged, lass."

He grazed her jaw with his fingertips. "The whoremonger took advantage of yer trusting nature and gentle heart."

Which was why Emily had wrapped both in an impenetrable, protective wall. Terrified she'd make the same stupid mistake again. Except now…she was older, wiser, and a good deal more cautious.

"Ye have nothing to be ashamed of, and any self-righteous prig who would judge ye when ye are the victim of a foul deed isn't worthy of your company."

Tobias squeezed her shoulder with his large palm, and sensation zipped along her nerve endings.

There was no sense denying his effect on her.

Not anymore.

To do so was futile.

Not only was Emily attracted to Tobias in a way she never believed herself capable of again, but he'd also managed to awaken something dormant in her heart.

"If the bugger were alive, I'd run the blackguard through and send him to the lowest level of hell where the vilest demons belong." Emotion rendered Tobias's voice rough and gravelly.

Emily adored him all the more for his chivalry.

She feared that the walls she'd so carefully erected and fortified all of these years were in danger of crumbling completely. Leaving her vulnerable and exposed.

Would that be so awful?

Yes. No.

She honestly didn't know.

Tobias pressed his lips to the crown of her head.

"Do not, for an instant, consider that I find ye at fault in any way, Emily, or that I would ban ye from Avery's presence. Ye've told the tale that ye have to protect yourself and Justina. I cannot fault ye for that."

Before Emily could respond, footsteps echoed in the corridor. She straightened and put a respectable distance between her and Tobias. He grabbed two sandwiches and scooted a foot away, where he disposed of the snack in short order.

The man certainly did like his sandwiches.

Pepperford entered, carrying a silver salver.

"A missive has arrived from Miss Levingtone. I presumed you might wish to read it at once, Your Grace."

"Thank you, Pepperford."

Tobias lifted the rectangle and, after breaking the dark green wax seal, swiftly read the contents.

The butler turned to Emily.

"Do you require anything, Mrs. Grenville? More hot tea? Almond biscuits?"

"No, but I thank you. Please tell the cook everything is delicious. The almond biscuits are some of the best I've ever tasted. So light and buttery. Simply scrumptious."

"She will be pleased to hear it." He offered a kindly smile, which gave him an elfin appearance, before departing at the same sedate pace he'd entered.

"It seems you've won over my butler, Emily. An

admirable feat, indeed."

"How so?" Flicking a crumb off her lap, she gave him an inquisitive glance.

After a furtive glance toward the door, Tobias leaned in and whispered, "Pepperford does *not* smile. There must be a ridiculous rule about majordomos needing to be stiff, pokery, solemn, and dignified." He winked. "To terrify the rest of us into doing their bidding."

She chuckled and set her serviette aside. "They do have a way of doing that, don't they? And knowing absolutely *everything* that goes on in the household."

Everything?

The thought rooted her to her seat.

Good Lord.

She sent a frantic look toward the empty doorway.

Pepperford couldn't have known she and Tobias had kissed.

Could he have?

Did that account for his genial manner toward her?

Saints above, did the majordomo erroneously believe there was something between her and Tobias?

There was a physical attraction, to be sure, but not anything more.

Nodding and oblivious to her inner turmoil, Tobias lifted the foolscap and gave it a short shake. "Avery is at the Duchess of San Sebastian's."

No surprise there.

Emily couldn't be happier that Avery was becoming such good friends with Justina. They were near in age, and neither had sisters. They filled a void in one another's lives, and it couldn't hurt Avery's chances for a successful launch into Society to have been befriended by multiple duchesses.

"After their outing, the women were chilled and decided tea was appropriate," he said.

In England, tea was always the answer.

"Reluctant to have their time together end, they've planned an impromptu dinner party. I am to consider this my invitation," Tobias said, laying the note aside. "Avery will borrow a gown from the duchess."

"I suppose it's not too soon to put our plan into play," Emily said. Pray to God it worked. "I'll schedule a modiste appointment for tomorrow."

She rose and shook out her skirts.

Sudden awkwardness engulfed her. She covered her discomfiture by donning her bonnet and gloves, then collecting her reticule.

She'd kissed this man like a wanton and then blurted her dirty little secret. A secret only Justina knew.

Tobias said he didn't condemn her, and Emily believed him.

Nonetheless, it would take time to forget the habits she'd forged over the years.

He unfolded and stood with that effortless masculine grace he possessed.

She liked that he was a big man: broad-shouldered, wide chest, biceps that strained the fabric of his coat, and thighs that flexed and rippled with muscles.

In contrast, Clement had been lean and sinewy.

"Until tonight." Tobias bowed over Emily's hand. "I *shall* count the hours."

Instead of sarcasm tinging his voice as it had the other day in Hyde Park, his tone rang with earnestness.

Her heart unfurled a smidgeon more.

"And Emily. Ye needn't worry that I'll reveal your past. Your secret is safe with me."

He wouldn't intentionally. Emily knew it to be true deep in her soul.

She searched his eyes, tender with sincerity.

"I know you shan't, Tobias."

On impulse, she stood on her toes and brushed his lips with hers. "Until tonight."

Then she fled.

What have I done?

Emily knew precisely what she'd done. Exactly what she'd vowed never to do.

Fallen in love.

The Theatre-Royal, Covent Garden

Two Weeks Later

Legs and arms crossed and a half-smile curving his mouth, Tobias leaned back into his chair in the corner of the Duke of Pennington's theater box. Pennington had generously offered his box to him and San Sebastian, neither of whom retained one as they spent most of their time in Scotland.

"Isn't it grand?" Avery leaned forward for a better view of the audience.

Ladies draped in the first stare of fashion fairly dripped in stunning jewels—although many of the pieces were likely paste or glass rather than gemstones. The gentlemen were only slightly less flamboyant with formal black, jeweled stickpins glittering in their neckcloths.

He and Emily had picked tonight for Avery's official, if somewhat late, introduction to Society. It had taken this long to see his niece appropriately garbed for the undertaking. Meanwhile, there had been numerous private dinners, outings to various attractions, rides in Hyde Park, strolls in Green Park, luncheons, and teas.

Baiting the hook, Emily had called it. Giving teasing glimpses of Avery here and there in the company of the *right* people. They'd succeeded in luring the *haut ton* into the net.

As Emily had intended, the upper salons buzzed with Avery's name.

Invitations had poured forth, satisfying in their numbers but also annoying, as Tobias loathed opening them.

Emily had come to his rescue, spending two mornings a week after their daily walks together. She sorted his correspondence, going through the invitations and setting aside those she deemed most beneficial for Avery to accept.

Tobias had been correct about ignoring the gossip rags. The top lofty denizens of High Society appeared to have eschewed the tattle of the Hyde Park incident. It helped that Lady Pooferhatch had run off with an Italian artist, after selling the family silver and jewels.

"Avery, don't gawk, dearest. Use your opera glasses," the Duchess of San Sebastian whispered surreptitiously from behind her fan. "Everyone stares—'tis expected. You mustn't, however, be obvious. It's considered gauche."

Yes, do stare, but don't be obvious in your gawping.

Avery unfurled her brisé fan and, waving it before her face, whispered back, "It would seem gaucheness is all the rage then."

She wasn't wrong.

From his vantage point in the shadows, Tobias observed several prestigious peers directing their opera glasses toward Pennington's box. More than one gentleman trained his lenses upon Emily.

Bloody blackguards.

Widows, particularly beautiful young widows, were always objects of licentious attention. Unexpected and foreign jealousy tunneled through Tobias's blood, stirring a possessiveness he refused to subdue.

Mine. She is mine.

Emily mightn't know it, and he couldn't formally claim her *yet*, but by holy God above, she *was* his. She would be his duchess if there was a God in heaven. After her confession a fortnight ago, she'd warmed to him significantly.

There'd been no more stolen kisses, not for his lack of desire. He'd caught Emily observing him numerous times, her hungry gaze dipping to his mouth before she averted her attention.

He was baiting the hook, and Emily was very close to taking the lure.

Clement Grenville was a bounder of the worst sort—God rot his unrepentant soul. When Tobias considered how Emily suffered, the fear, humiliation, and poverty that had shadowed her for over a decade, it cleaved his heart in two.

If she would permit him to, he'd show her what it meant to be truly loved and adored. Cherished and revered. She'd never know another second's humiliation as his duchess.

Still, he would not rush her. Patience and persistence were his weapons.

Eyes alight with excitement, Avery clutched his arm.

"Isn't it magnificent, Uncle?"

Was this elegant, polished young woman truly the same imp who'd run barefoot through the fields at Ballyleigh Court? Who'd fought him tooth and nail to stay in Scotland and had loudly and vehemently condemned his soul to Hades for forcing her to come to London?

Any doubt that she'd be a success, a diamond of the first water, had dissipated. Although, if the young blades wanted to keep their teeth and sport unblackened eyes, they'd best look upon her with respect and nothing else.

"Uncle?"

Tobias realized he hadn't answered Avery.

"It is indeed remarkable."

His gaze strayed to Emily, positively radiant in a silver and ice-blue gown overlaid with pearl-studded white lace. Her upswept hair revealed an alabaster throat, and the sapphire and diamond jewels at her ears, throat, and wrist sparkled and twinkled from the light of hundreds of candles.

She was all that was perfection and goodness. As beautiful in character and personality as she was in outward appearance.

Tobias was convinced he couldn't love her any more, yet his love grew exponentially every day. That was the remarkable thing about love; there was no limit to love's depth, width, or breadth. The heart and soul could accommodate an unlimited amount.

"Now *you're* staring, Heatherston." Wry humor colored San Sebastian's murmured words, meant for Tobias's ears alone. "When are ye going to do something about it?"

Tobias didn't have to ask what "*it*" was. He'd been friends with San Sebastian too long to pretend ignorance. Tobias cast him a sidelong look before resting his attention on Emily once more. "She needs time."

"Justina has never revealed precisely what troubles her aunt." San Sebastian crossed his legs, his gaze penetrating but not prying. "But I have the utmost admiration for Emily and would see her happy and content."

"That is my intention as well." If Tobias had his way, she'd never know unhappiness, insecurity, or trepidation again.

As if sensing she was the subject of their discussion, Emily glanced in their direction. Her gaze swung between them, a tiny crease between her eyebrows.

Tobias lifted his glass of champagne in a silent toast to her, and a brilliant smile blossomed across her face before Justina said something and drew her attention away.

"Well, well, well." Grinning like a stray cat who'd discovered a saucer of warm cream, San Sebastian raised his flute. "I'd say felicitations will be in order sooner rather than later, my friend."

Tobias prayed his San Sebastian was right. His future happiness depended upon it. Nevertheless, he was a patient man.

What was that adage?

The best things were worth waiting for?

He'd wait as long as it took for Emily to come to love him.

The production began, and the audience settled in to watch the performance of…

Devil a bit.

What *were* they watching?

Had anyone told Tobias?

If so, he couldn't recall.

A small, secretive smile arching her mouth, Emily glanced his way before focusing on the stage.

If his life depended on it, he couldn't have told a soul what the play was about. He should have observed Avery, but his deuced regard repeatedly gravitated to Emily. Until, at last, he stopped fighting against the temptation and simply relished watching her.

Intermission arrived much too soon, and he dragged his focus from her to the rows of boxes across from them. The enigmatic Cortland Marlow-Westbrook, heir presumptive to the Elridge earldom, sat directly across from them. His dark eyes hooded and contemplative, Marlow-Westbrook regarded Avery with something more than passing interest.

Marlow-Westbrook's gaze swung to Tobias, and the young blood cocked an eyebrow, a wry smile skewing his mouth.

He rose and exited his box.

Tobias would bet Spiorad that the gentleman, known for his horsemanship and sharp, cutting wit, made his way to Pennington's box at this very minute to beg an introduction to Avery.

Tobias didn't know Marlow-Westbrook well. However, the man had a reputation for fairness, and no unsavory habits were linked to his name.

Avery could do far worse than an heir to an earldom.

Still, the choice would be hers, and Tobias would not rush his niece. If she didn't want to marry until she was thirty, it was her life. He'd been deliberately obtuse in leaking the precise amount of her dowry to avoid attracting fortune hunters.

The ladies excused themselves to use the necessary.

Tobias stood to stretch his legs and braced himself for the usual onslaught of curious *le beau monde* members venturing forth to meet Avery.

The first of the inquisitive *ton* made Pennington's box before the ladies returned, including Cortland Marlow-Westbrook.

"Heatherston. San Sebastian." Marlow-Westbrook dipped his chin, his keen gaze astute and alert.

"Marlow-Westbrook," San Sebastian replied.

"I presume you wish an introduction to my niece?" Tobias leveled the man twelve years his junior with a severe glance.

Clasping his hands behind his back and rocking back on his heels, the younger man shook his head. "That's not why I am here, though naturally, I would be well pleased to meet her. Since returning to London last week, I've heard much about the remarkable Miss Levingtone."

His unexpected response took Tobias aback.

Had he misjudged the man's interest in Avery?

"There are a slew of Grenvilles on my mother's side," Marlow-Westbrook offered by way of further explanation. "I'm curious to learn if Mrs. Grenville married a relative."

Blister and blast.

After all this time, someone had taken note of Emily's surname?

Probably because of the notoriety Avery was receiving, and Emily's name had been linked with hers. Or, perhaps it was indeed as simple as Marlow-Westbrook's return to England recently. The chap had toured the continent as many young bucks were wont to do.

Every muscle in Tobias stiffened in alarm. He forced himself to relax and bent his mouth into a friendly arc. "I wasn't aware you were related to any Grenvilles, though the name is common enough."

He prayed that was the case.

"True. Most people associate the surname with George Grenville, as he was the prime minister. My mother is descended from one of George Grenville's paternal uncles, and she has numerous Grenville cousins. They are a prolific lot." He chuckled and adjusted his cuff. "Rather like the Westbrooks."

Tobias swore an extremely foul oath inside his head. This was the last thing Emily needed. It might well be enough to cause her to flee London. Even England.

Consternation etched San Sebastian's features as his keen gaze snared with Tobias's.

Perceptive man. He'd ascertained something was afoot.

The sounds of women laughing and chatting carried to them before Emily, Avery, the Duchess of San Sebastian, and the Dukes and Duchesses of Sutcliffe and Westfall crowded into the box.

San Sebastian took it upon himself to introduce Marlow-Westbrook to Emily and Avery.

They greeted him politely, and Avery blushed prettily when he bowed over her hand.

Tobias hadn't been off his mark after all.

Rising from a well-executed bow, Marlow-Westbrook homed in on Emily.

Tobias encircled her elbow with his hand, giving a gentle squeeze. An urgent warning. But how could she possibly understand his silent message?

She cast him an inquisitive glance and drew her brows together.

Ah, she comprehended something was wrong. At least there was that.

"Mrs. Grenville?" Marlow-Westbrook said, drawing her attention from Tobias. "I believe we might be related. My mother was a Grenville."

Good God above.

Emily flashed hot, then cold, then hot again. A thousand drums echoed inside her head, hammering a vicious cadence behind her eyes.

Tobias had tried to warn her.

That's why he'd taken her arm and given a slight squeeze, silently speaking to her with his potent gaze.

She sought his eyes, unprepared for the stark concern she saw glimmering there.

This was bad. Very, very bad.

What had Mr. Marlow-Westbrook said to him?

After all of this time, her worst fears had come to pass.

For the first time in her life, she was sorely tempted

to fake a swoon. Acutely aware that every person in the theater box gazed at her expectedly, she marshaled her composure and fashioned what she hoped would pass for a genial smile.

"I doubt it, Mr. Marlow-Westbrook. I didn't meet my husband in England."

Emily wasn't about to divulge anything more to the inquisitive man.

She pressed two fingers to her forehead. She mightn't faint, but the megrim that attacked her skull with the force of a blacksmith's anvil was very real indeed.

"Aunt Emily?" Justina, the dear girl, recognized the symptoms at once. She touched Emily's other arm. "Is it one of your megrims?"

"I fear so," Emily managed, sounding far frailer than she liked. She swallowed, nausea billowing up her throat. She might very well cast up her accounts. Wouldn't that give that toadying troll of a reporter something to write about?

She closed her eyes, willing the sickness to pass.

These sudden onset headaches were the worst.

They gave Emily no time to prepare. To take headache powders, don her nightclothes, and lie down in a dark room with a cold cloth across her head.

"San Sebastian, might I impose upon you to bring Avery home when the performance is over?" Tobias asked, taking charge.

Good. He'd know what to do.

Remaining upright took all of Emily's concentration.

"Not a bit of it," Justina said. "We shall all depart. I am most familiar with my aunt's megrims. I must go with her. I am sorry, Avery. There will be other performances."

"Please do not apologize," Avery said. "Naturally, we must see Mrs. Grenville home at once."

The others in the box offered polite sympathies as Justina and Avery gathered their things.

"I hope you recover swiftly, Mrs. Grenville," Mr. Marlow-Westbrook said, genuine compassion in his eyes.

"Thank you." Emily couldn't even summon a wan smile, so lightheaded and dizzy was she.

With every passing minute, she truly feared she might be sick.

She swallowed again, striving for equanimity.

Not here. Not in front of all of these people.

She had no doubt that dozens of opera glasses were pointed in their direction even now.

With Justina on one side and Avery on the other, Emily took an unsteady step forward, then another.

Tobias made a rough sound in his throat. "Permit me, please."

He scooped Emily into his arms, and with a sigh, she closed her eyes and pillowed her head against the broad, comforting expanse of his chest. She'd face the humiliation tomorrow. But at this moment, she needed him.

Sweet Jesus, her head hurt.

What am I going to do about Mr. Marlow-Westbrook?

Emily's perfidy had finally caught up with her.

~*~

Houghtenwick Hall – Grosvenor Square

The next morning – a few minutes past eleven

You're a coward, Emily Grenville.

Today Emily felt spineless, and she wouldn't apologize or feel guilty about it, either. That proverb about wisdom being the better part of valor definitely applied in her circumstances.

Her needlework lying idly in her lap, she gazed through the spotless drawing room window to the garden. May had arrived in a gloriously colorful palette and a temperament much more benevolent than April's.

Emily had skipped her constitutional and sent a note 'round to Tobias begging off their regular morning meeting.

Yes, she had taken the coward's way.

Fear of having one's sins exposed rather brought out the least admirable characteristics in a person.

When Emily had not come down for breakfast, Justina had popped into her bedchamber. She'd attributed Emily's absence in the dining room to the lingering aftermath of the megrim. They'd plagued Emily often enough during Justina's youth that she was familiar with Emily's recovery, and Justina had assumed such was the case today.

Hopefully, Tobias would come to the same conclusion.

The plain truth was that Emily was terrified of running into Mr. Marlow-Westbrook on her outing. Instead, she'd planned a day at home, donned one of her older morning gowns—a simple white affair with a crocheted fichu for modesty—and thrown a knitted crimson shawl that had seen better days around her shoulders before venturing to the drawing room.

This morning, Justina and Avery had planned a visit to the milliners with Ophelia, the Duchess of Asherford. Ophelia picked them up in her black lacquered coach, and Baxter had left early for a meeting.

Emily had the house to herself, except for the servants, of course.

After bringing her a tray of tea and toast, Bevels had left her to her own devices.

In truth, her headache had abated during the early morning hours. She'd lain in her wickedly comfortable bed and played through scenario after scenario in her mind of the possible repercussions of her perfidy being revealed.

None ended pleasantly or with her remaining in London.

Precisely where did Mr. Marlow-Westbrook perch in Clement's family tree?

Emily knew scant few details about her dead husband except that he had been married and fathered three children.

More fool she, for following her heart and not her head.

Had Clement any siblings?

Where was he from? Well, naturally, he was from England, but *where* exactly?

Were his parents still alive?

When had the bugger tossed aside all decency and morality?

Such details a couple ought to learn about one another *before* exchanging vows. In hindsight, Emily realized Clement had been rather close-mouthed about many things, which was why she'd been given to speculating he was a spy. Now, she conceded he may have simply been afraid to divulge too much about himself.

The craven coward.

In point of fact, Emily conceded she'd been at fault too. Orphaned as a young child and a burden to a stuffy older brother, she'd yearned for love and affection.

A coal tit landed on a lilac branch, the lavender blooms on the cusp of blooming. The bird artfully balanced despite the capricious breeze ruffling its feathers.

The urge to pack her belongings in the wee morning hours and escape in Baxter's coach to her cottage in Bristol had tempted Emily greatly. To be perfectly honest, she still hadn't utterly dismissed that possibility.

Leaving would be best for Justina and Avery, she told herself.

But Emily's love for Tobias wouldn't let her sneak off. At least not without saying farewell first.

He deserved that.

She deserved that.

Undoubtedly, her offer of employment as a companion would be rescinded if and when the ugly truth of her deception became known.

She bit the fingernail of her forefinger in the manner she had as a small child.

Marlow-Westbrook mightn't be related to Clement.

Yet, instinct told her he was. There was a faint familial resemblance around his eyes and his jawline.

Her ruse had finally come to its expected ruinous end.

Honestly, Emily fretted more about how her lies would affect Avery and Justina. Baxter and Tobias wouldn't feel the brunt of the censure. Men rarely did.

Dukes *never* did.

The least selfish, wisest thing was to leave.

Now.

While everyone was away.

She put her fist to her mouth to still the animalistic cry that hurtled to the front of her mouth.

It wasn't fair.

None of this was Emily's fault. The injustice coiled deep in her belly, bitter and hot.

The pain she'd experienced when Clement had abandoned her was a mere scratch compared to the agony cleaving her in two at the thought of leaving Tobias. To never see his beloved face again. Never hear the rich timbre of his brogue. Never, ever, feel his arms around her or his lips upon hers.

A fat, warm teardrop landed on her other hand, and

she stared at it in surprise.

She hadn't even realized she'd begun weeping. Swiping at the offending moisture, she willed the tears to stop.

Setting aside her needlework, she rose.

Emily knew what she must do. What the right thing to do was.

A soft rap upon the door drew her attention.

Bevels stood there in all of his dignified fustiness.

"Mrs. Grenville, the Duke of Heatherston has called. Are you at home?"

Emily's heart leaped for joy and then promptly plummeted to her slippers.

Tobias was here.

Too late, her heart cried.

It was too late. Too late to declare her love. Too late to seize what he'd offered her all of those months ago.

"Yes, Bevels. Please show him in."

So Emily could tell him goodbye.

As Tobias waited in the foyer, he half-expected Bevels to return and tell him Emily wasn't receiving callers. He assumed her headache yet plagued her, and compassion for her suffering gripped him. She'd been so pale and fragile last night.

Frightened too, although one had to look closely to see the dread behind the pain in her tumultuous eyes.

Tobias couldn't help but conclude the shock of Marlow-Westbrook's question had contributed to the extremeness of her megrim.

Bevels trod down the corridor, his expression inscrutable.

"Mrs. Grenville will receive you in the drawing room, Your Grace."

She wasn't abed. Excellent news.

Tobias had timed his visit to coincide with Avery and Justina's outing. He wanted to speak to Emily alone. If she was up to receiving callers, that was.

"I'll announce myself, Bevels."

Bevels' grizzled eyebrows flexed the merest bit, the only hint of his disapproval.

"Very good, Your Grace."

The butler's tone indicated it was anything but very good.

At the drawing room entrance, Tobias permitted himself the pleasure of gazing at Emily. As she had his first visit, she stood before the window, her expression contemplative.

She must've sensed his presence, for she slowly turned.

The bleakness and resignation in her beautiful eyes rendered him speechless for an instant.

She was leaving.

There was no need for her to speak the words aloud.

He saw it in her eyes, felt it in his cracking heart.

Tobias's soul howled an anguished *No*.

He had no doubt she'd only received him to tell him goodbye.

Bollocks to that.

He wouldn't let her run away—wouldn't permit that miserable wretch Grenville to take anything more from her. To steal their chance for love and happiness.

In a trice, Tobias strode across the room and gathered her into his arms.

"*Mo ghrádh*, my love," he murmured into her perfumed hair.

She smelled of lemons and vanilla and Emily.

His precious, darling, selfless Emily.

Tilting her head, she opened her mouth, tears of regret shimmering in her eyes.

Putting a forefinger to the soft pillows of her lips, he shook his head.

"Nae, lass. Nae."

Tobias kissed her forehead, marking her as his for all time.

"I shan't let ye rob us both because of your misplaced sense of duty. Ye've sacrificed enough, *leannan*." He closed his eyes, his words an invocation to the Almighty, a prayer and petition, as much as they were an oath to her.

"I vow to protect ye with my life. I love ye, Emily. I wish to make ye my duchess."

He angled away from her, searching her dear, sweet, tear-dampened face.

Her eyes, framed by a fringe of spiky lashes, grew wide, and she clamped her lower lip between her teeth.

"I ken ye are afraid, darling, but with me by your side, ye needn't ever fear again. I shall never leave ye. *Never*."

"Oh, Tobias." Such sadness and despair ravaged her features, his gut clenched as if he'd been impaled. "But is our love enough?"

His heart soared to heaven.

Emily loved him.

He'd be bound she didn't even realize she'd said it, but it was sufficient for him. For now.

She drew in a shuddery breath. "The scandal…"

"I don't give two farthings about a scandal, and neither does Avery. Or Justina or San Sebastian or any of our other friends. You do us a great disservice if you think any of us would turn our backs on ye because ye trusted a blackguard and he betrayed ye."

"He's right, you know."

Emily gasped, her dainty mouth slack as she and Tobias faced the doorway.

San Sebastian filled the entrance, but no censure marred his features at catching them in an embrace.

"Baxter… I." Emily sent Tobias a helpless look but didn't step from his arms.

His blood sang through his veins at the concession.

In that minutest way, she'd accepted she was his, even if unconsciously.

Curving his mouth into a gentle smile, San Sebastian advanced further into the room.

"I don't know what your secret is, Emily. My wife has never revealed it, and we share everything. She says it's yours to share when you're ready. You are family, Emily, and we will get through whatever this is together."

"Ahem." Bevels cleared his throat.

That was another eerie quality of majordomos— that ability to appear out of thin air.

"You have another caller, Mrs. Grenville. Mr. Cortland Marlow-Westbrook."

"The bugger didn't wait long," Tobias muttered, itching to have a word with the good fellow before Emily did.

Why was Marlow-Westbrook so determined to uncover the truth? Like a bloody hound on the scent of a fox.

Emily glanced between him and San Sebastian. "I'll see him. Let's have this done once and for all."

"As you wish," the butler said deferentially.

Bevels departed, and as they waited for Marlow-Westbrook to be shown in, they seated themselves. Tobias claimed the cushion beside Emily on the closest settee while San Sebastian chose a nearby armchair.

Tobias took Emily's hand in his, and she turned a grateful gaze upon him.

They would get through this together.

"Mr. Marlow-Westbrook," Bevels intoned with the same enthusiasm as an executioner announcing a death sentence.

The first crack of fashion in a scarlet coat, gold,

black, and claret waistcoat, and a frothy neckcloth from whence a ruby stickpin glittered, Marlow-Westbrook gave a shallow bow.

"Please have a tea tray prepared, Bevels," Emily said, falling into the role of hostess with natural adeptness despite her unease.

With a nod, the butler departed.

"Good morning." Marlow-Westbrook didn't seem the least taken aback to find Tobias and San Sebastian also present.

The men exchanged perfunctory greetings.

"Please do have a seat, Mr. Marlow-Westbrook," Emily said, withdrawing her hand from Tobias's.

Marlow-Westbrook sank onto the opposite settee. "I hope you are quite recovered from your headache, Mrs. Grenville."

His gaze was a trifle too keen for mere politesse.

"I am." Emily folded her hands in her lap, clenching them tightly.

Such a brave darling.

"Last night, you inquired about my late husband, Mr. Marlow-Westbrook."

Angling his dark head in the affirmative, Marlow-Westbrook said, "I did. My mother has several Grenville cousins. You mentioned you didn't meet in England."

"We did not. My brother was a diplomat until his passing. It was he who introduced me to Lieutenant Clement Grenville."

Tobias waited for Marlow-Westbrook's reaction.

It took all of two heartbeats.

Disbelief whisked across the young man's features as he stiffened and his jaw tightened. No doubt the severity of Emily's accusations hit the target straight on. "But...Clement Grenville had a wife and family in Essex."

"So I learned when he abandoned me." With estimable poise and composure, Emily repeated the unsavory tale she'd told Tobias a fortnight ago.

San Sebastian's expression grew ever more flint-like and enraged, while Marlow-Westbrook's remained rigid, his face impassive.

"So there you have it in all of its tawdry truth," Emily said.

"What tawdry truth?" The Duchess of San Sebastian glided into the drawing room, Avery at her heels.

Emily winced but, to her credit, notched her rounded chin up an inch.

Never had Tobias known such a courageous woman, and his love for her threatened to explode his heart.

With an eye on Avery, Emily chose her words with care. "I have just shared with Mr. Marlow-Westbrook how I came to be Mrs. Clement Grenville."

At once, the duchess's welcoming smile vanished, and she went to stand behind her aunt. Placing a hand on Emily's shoulder in a protective gesture, she narrowed her eyes. "And pray tell, why would *you* need to know *that*, Mr. Marlow-Westbrook?"

"He was second or third cousin to my mother," he responded stiffly. "I thought Mrs. Grenville might like to become acquainted with the rest of the family."

"Hardly," her grace scoffed with such contempt, Marlow-Westbrook flushed.

Completely befuddled but sensing something was

amiss, Avery looked between the other four adults in the room.

Marlow-Westbrook skimmed his avid gaze over Avery, and she offered him a demure smile.

Definitely sparks between those two, but Tobias wasn't as keen to welcome the man's suit after this interlude. Might never be, depending on the outcome today, truth be told.

With what might have been remorse, Marlow-Westbrook pointed his attention to Emily.

"Mrs. Grenville, I sincerely regret any upset my visit has caused you." Marlow-Westbrook stood, and something very near consternation shadowed his features. "I think it is best for all if this matter is never discussed again."

Emily canted her head. "*I* certainly shall never do so."

She'd clearly and cleverly told him that if the gossipmongers caught wind of it, it would be because of indiscretion on his part. The gossips would be equally malicious to the real Mrs. Clement Grenville and her children as they would to Emily, and he knew it.

"I've taken enough of your time." After a brief bow, Marlow-Westbrook quit the room.

Face pinched in puzzlement, Avery plunked her hands on her hips. "Will someone *please* tell me what is going on?"

Mayhap someday, Avery would know the sordid tale, but not today. Instead, Tobias grinned and grasped Emily's hand.

"I have proposed to Emily."

Avery squealed and rushed to embrace her. "I'm so very glad. I knew there was something between you two that day first in the park."

"Congratulations," San Sebastian said. "Good to know you took my advice, Heatherston.'"

Justina bent down and wrapped her arms around her aunt's neck. "I couldn't be more delighted for you, Aunt Emily."

"I haven't said yes."

Everyone's attention shot to Emily as an unnatural silence spun out far too long.

Tobias's heart stalled, the pain stabbing his chest worse than the broken rib he endured. Surely she didn't still intend to leave?

"*Leannan*?"

She met his gaze, hers clear and bright and, for the first time, unfettered by the shadows that had haunted her since they'd first met.

"You didn't propose, Tobias. You said you loved me and *wanted* to marry me. That is not a proposal. It is a statement."

"Poorly done, old chap." San Sebastian couldn't keep the hilarity from his voice. "I could've given you a pointer or two if I'd known what a debacle you'd make of it."

"Uncle Tobias." Avery scowled. "Do you even have a ring?"

Feeling very much a chastised lad, he shook his head. "Not with me."

He hadn't come intending to propose.

The ring sat in the top right desk drawer.

She threw her hands in the air. "When the day comes that I am proposed to, if my beloved botches it as badly as you have, I shall say no."

"Might I suggest we leave Aunt Emily and Tobias alone so that..." An incredulous expression flitted across Justina's face. "Why, Avery. I've just realized. My aunt shall also be *your* aunt and your uncle, *my* uncle."

"It's the grandest thing!" Avery clapped her hands. "We shall be cousins."

Emily bent her mouth into a tolerant smile. "I *still* haven't said yes."

"Oh, yes. Of course," Justina said, still beaming. "Let's allow them a moment of privacy."

Chattering like magpies, Justina and Avery left the drawing room, arm in arm.

San Sebastian followed at a more sedate pace. He tossed over his shoulder, "Welcome to the family, Heatherston."

Emily peaked her eyebrows high on her forehead. "I haven't said…"

"*Yes*." San Sebastian chuckled and pulled his earlobe. "I know. I know. I shall leave you to it then."

Tobias didn't wait until the door snicked closed. He pulled Emily onto his lap and captured her mouth in a searing kiss.

"Marry me, Emily. Please marry me. Ye must say

yes, lass. I don't want to live my life without ye. Ye've filled my heart with joy unimagined."

Eyes bright with love, she placed her palm on his cheek.

"Yes, you dear, sweet, patient, tolerant, kind, loving man. I will be your wife, and I can only pray that I make you as happy as you've made me."

"Aye, I've no doubt ye will." He winked. "Did I mention I want a large family?"

"Then I suppose a short betrothal is in order," Emily said, with a mischievous spark in her eye. "I am past my prime, you know."

"I believe I can persuade ye otherwise, my love."

And he did. Most handily.

# Epilogue

The Duke and Duchess of Sutcliffe's
20 May 1811— Evening

Never had Emily been this happy, and tonight, surrounded by her dearest friends, she and Tobias would formally announce their betrothal. After, of course, Victor, Duke of Sutcliffe, had been honored for his birthday celebration.

Rather than sitting with the dowagers, companions, chaperones, and wallflowers as had been her wont these past several years, Emily whirled across the sanded dance floor in Tobias's arms. It was glorious to feel alive once more—to be able to truly enjoy life.

"You're smiling again, my love," Tobias murmured

into her ear, his breath a hot caress that sent a tingle down her spine.

Emily tilted her head to meet his heated gaze.

"I cannot seem to stop, Tobias. I'm so happy."

"As am I," he said when the cotillion steps brought them together again. "People have taken note. I doubt we need to announce our betrothal. Only a muttonhead wouldn't realize we are in love."

In love.

How she rejoiced at hearing him say it. For having the chance to love this remarkable man. That though she'd despaired of ever finding happiness, God had granted her heart's desire.

Emily glanced around, returning Theadosia, Duchess of Sutcliffe's, warm smile from across the ballroom where she danced with her husband, Victor. The Earl of Wainthorpe raised his champagne glass before bending his neck to listen to something his wife, Bianca, said.

Several guests observed the dancers, and Emily and Tobias garnered particular attention. Emily, a widow, had snatched up one of the few remaining eligible dukes, and not every gaze directed toward her was congratulatory.

Emily didn't care.

She no longer needed to fret about what others thought or that her *secret* might be discovered.

Standing together on one side, the Earls of Scarborough and Keyworth chatted with the Dukes of Sheffield, Bainbridge, and Dandridge. No doubt their ladies had sought the retiring room *en masse*.

Justina and Baxter, James and Regine Brentwood, the Duke and Duchess of Westfall, and the Duke and Duchess of Kincade comprised one of the cotillion quartets. Asherford, Waycross, and Pennington and their duchesses completed the set Emily and Tobias danced in.

The hundred or so exclusive guests were here to celebrate Victor, Duke of Sutcliffe's birthday. Not precisely an intimate group, but assuredly genial and consisting mostly of close friends and family. Emily couldn't remember the last time she'd attended a *ton* event, any event, and felt at ease.

And it was all because of the tall, strong, handsome,

and ever-so-loving man at her side.

With a flourish, the musicians brought the dance to an end. Emily curtsied, and Tobias bowed. At once, Tobias took her elbow. "You're flushed, my darling. Let's get something cool to drink."

"Yes, please."

The unseasonably warm day had turned into a rather hot evening. Even with the ballroom doors to the terrace wide open, the room was overly hot.

At the refreshment table, a footman handed Emily a glass of ratafia and Tobias a glass of punch.

Expression animated, Avery approached. She was stunning in a white gown with a pink over robe, and pearls and flowers woven into her dark curls. "I truly didn't think I'd enjoy a Season, but your friends are so kind and helpful."

Tobias skimmed his gaze over the crowd, and a smile notched his firm mouth up on one side.

"They are. We are fortunate that our circle consists of honorable and honest people of integrity. Much of *le beau monde* is not."

"*Le beau monde* is not what?" Jessica, Duchess of Bainbridge, asked with a smile.

"Kind. Decent. Honorable," Avery offered with an impish grin.

"Ah." Jessica knew firsthand just how unpleasant the rich and powerful could be. She linked her arm with Avery's. "That's why, my dear, we stick together." She angled her head to include several of their friends who had come near. "We're more than friends and family. We're comrades, brethren."

"Hear, hear," Nicolette, the Duchess of Westfall, agreed.

Standing near the musicians, her husband at her side, the Duchess of Sutcliffe clapped her hands. "May I have everyone's attention, please?"

Slowly the buzz of voices quieted as the guests faced her grace.

"I wish to propose a toast before passing through to supper," Theadosia said. "If you don't have a beverage, please select one from a servant."

A few moments ticked on as those who didn't have a glass acquired one.

Theadosia lifted her glass. "To my beloved husband on his birthday. Long life and health."

A chorus of "Hear, hears" and "Huzzahs" filled the air.

When the din subsided, Sutcliffe raised his flute. "Thank you for all of your well-wishes and felicitations. You've made this birthday one I shall long remember. A toast to loyal and true friends, both old and new."

Another round of cheers went up.

Tobias wrapped his arm around Emily's waist and whispered in her ear. "And here's to a lifetime with the most remarkable woman. The love of my life, the keeper of my heart, and my very own soulmate."

Untold joy filled her as she touched her glass to his.

"To us, my love. For now and always."

USA Today Bestselling, award-winning author COLLETTE CAMERON® scribbles Scottish and Regency historicals featuring dashing rogues and scoundrels and the intrepid damsels who reform them. Blessed with an overactive and witty muse that won't stop whispering new romantic romps in her ear, she's lived in Oregon her entire life, though she dreams of living in Scotland part-time. A self-confessed Cadbury chocoholic, you'll always find a dash of inspiration and a pinch of humor in her sweet-to-spicy timeless romances®.

Explore **Collette's worlds** at
collettecameron.com!

Join her **VIP Reader Club** and **FREE newsletter**.
Giggles guaranteed!

FREE BOOK: Join Collette's The Regency Rose®
VIP Reader Club to get updates on book releases, cover
reveals, contests, and giveaways she reserves
exclusively for email and newsletter followers. Also,
any deals, sales, or special promotions are offered to
club members first. She will not share your name or
email, nor will she spam you.

http://bit.ly/TheRegencyRoseGift

Follow Collette on BookBub
www.bookbub.com/authors/collette-cameron

Thank you for reading WHEN A DUKE DESIRES A LASS. I hope you've enjoyed the last installment in my SEDUCTIVE SCOUNDRELS series.

As with all good things, the series has come to an end. I'm both sad and excited. It's always hard to say goodbye to good friends, but I have a new series I can't wait to dive into writing. Look for the first installment of the Chronicles of the Westbrook Brides in 2023.

To ensure you don't miss it, the next round of the *Wicked Earls Club*, or my other book news, subscribe to *The Regency Rose*, my newsletter (Get a free ebook too!) at collettecameron.com. I also have a fabulous VIP Reader Group on Facebook. If you're a fan of my books and historical romance, I'd love to have you join me. You'll also be the first to see new covers, read exclusive excerpts, be the first to know about contests and giveaways, help me pick titles and name characters, and much, much more!

Please consider telling other readers why you

enjoyed this book by reviewing it. I also truly adore hearing from my readers. You can contact me at collettecameron.com and explore my author world while there. If you enjoy reading sweet historical Christian romances, check out my DAUGHTERS OF DESIRE series. You'll see a few familiar characters from the SEDUCTIVE SCOUNDRELS series.

Hugs,

Collette

A Lady, a Kiss, a Christmas Wish

Daughters of Desire (Scandalous Ladies), Book One

Sometimes you have to take a few risks on the road to happily ever after…

He dared to defy tradition…

Lord Brandon Morrisette is a born risk-taker. Instead of claiming his place in society, he became a physician to help the less fortunate. So, when he sees a patient mistreating her sweet, bright-eyed companion, Brandon is determined to help bring some holiday cheer into the poor girl's life. It's the least he can do. But in truth, he'd like to do much more for the kind-hearted beauty who so easily captured his attention…and his heart.

She guards a scandalous secret…

Joy Winterborne can't afford to take risks. If anyone found out about her past, she'd lose everything. And getting fired from her companion job would deprive her of the only bright spot in her otherwise dreary life—the time she gets to spend with the charming and oh-so-handsome Dr. Morrisette. Of course, nothing can ever come of her attraction to him. He's nobility, and she's nobody. But that doesn't stop her silly heart from wanting…*more.*

With a little luck, some mistletoe, and maybe even a Christmas wish, can Brandon convince Joy to take the greatest risk of all—falling in love?